I0536872

46

15

53

PANDORA PRESS

46 15 53
Copyright © 2013 Pandora Press
ISBN: 978-0615848198

Pandora Press
15351 Hwy 5
Cabot, AR 72023

Kelvin Cornelius,
I started this for me,
and finished it for you.
It's all yours, brother.

TABLE OF CONTENTS

TABLE OF CONTENTS

46

15

53

"For this corruptible must put on incorruption, and this mortal *must* put on immortality.
So when this corruptible shall have put on incorruption, and this mortal shall have put on
immortality, then shall be brought to pass the saying that is written,
Death is swallowed up in victory.

1 Corinthians 15:53-54 — KJV

They're funny little things, scurrying around in the dark, holding out for hope. It strikes a chord, how the weakest of things can be the most cherished, and the strongest despised.

Eyes of Eternity roam the earth, searching, longing, keening...they are beautiful. But beautiful forever is not enough. Oh, for one fleeting moment of transience, one occurrence to look back on and say "it was wrong".

Will it ever be realized that it is better to breathe for one tainted, glorious moment of impulse, than to languish in perfect harmony? If only, only to stray from the path, to do as others have done—to hold our lives in our hands, breathe our own breath, speak our own words. To love our own loves.

But no. Not here. Not yet anyway. The sky is yet to be set screaming with revolution, the moon yet to be turned to blood. Those days are coming. I am watching and I have found my Messiah. So does the world unturn. So angels fall from heaven.

Elven Woes – Kieran

"Mother, this is insane." I protested, watching her bright eyes examine varying shades of paint.

"Hush, child." she scolded. "Planning a nursery is not something to take lightly. Choice of color is very impacting on a baby's development. We have to choose just the right one."

On cue, two nauseating shades of pink were thrust before my eyes.

"Do you like these?"

"It would be wretched and hideous splashed on walls."

My mother had the gall to look offended. "Really, Kieran? Don't you think you should be more invested in the life of your baby?"

"I'm not pregnant!" I yelled, not caring that people paused and stared. "And I'm not married."

My mother put on her long-suffering mask and smiled. "But you will be in a week. And then there will be children."

My temper bubbled. "Mother, I am not getting married in a week."

"Kieran, the match has been arranged since before you were born. It's your duty to your people."

"My people can deal." I quipped. "Being elven isn't everything, and the cloying traditions are a pain in my ass!"

"Kieran!" my mother paled in horror. "How dare you say such a thing!?"

In an attempt at normalcy, I turned my attention to the paint colors. "I dare because I'm fed up." I answered.

Mother opened her mouth again, I assumed to chastise me, when two young women, smelling faintly of cinnamon, walked by the aisle. Mom gasped and huddled along the edge of the wall.

"Ancestors protect us." she breathed. "Kieran, cover your ears."

"It's a human run establishment, mom." I huffed. "Even witches won't try anything. Relax."

Sorrow filled my mother's eyes. "Do you not remember what they did to you? How recently this new treaty has come into effect?"

I put a hand to the corner of my eye, tracing the rather noticeable scar that snaked out over my cheekbone and down to my jaw line. There were worse marks under my clothes. "I remember. I remember and I don't care. The only reason nothing changes is because we don't let it."

"Why are you so angry today, Kieran?" how she managed to sound bewildered was beyond me.

I sighed. Most elven women made it their life's mission to fall in love with the one chosen for them and spend their happy elven lives having happy elven children so that happy elven grandparents could hand down a legacy of distorted lore, racism, and bloodshed. It was a horrid cycle; one in which I wanted no part.

"Because are world is so flawed, even the flaws are screwed up." I answered, trying to turn down my anger.

"Don't tell me about our flawed world." she warned, her sparkling eyes fading into hell. "Not until you have your daughter brought home to you, broken and bleeding, barely clinging onto life and…"

I wrapped her in a tight hug and held her close to me. "I know. I'm so sorry, mom."

"It's okay, baby." she answered. "I'm here and you're here. And those days are over."

Misgiving burned through me again as I thought of the letter sitting at home…on the same table as my unwanted wedding dress. How did I tell her? How did I tell any of my people that those days weren't over? That, maybe, they were about to become much worse, on a much larger scale?

I couldn't. I smiled, watching my mother scan paint colors. Weddings could wait, bad news could wait. Hell. Even heaven could wait.

"Mia Redblade, the coven finds you…"

Silence hung in thah aih like my future, on a very tense thread. Sweat tickled as it slid down my back. *Finds me what?*

Thah aih electrahfied with shock, horrah, an' awe. Everybody's auras lit up like fuckin' fireflies. Angah coiled in my shouldahs an' settled to a gnawin' ache. Thah only thing hurtin' worse than thah twist in my gut was thah look on my mothah's face.

Here's your gal, ma. Sorry she's a sucktastic daughtah…an' witch.

"Does the defendant have any last words to say before the coven pronounces their sentence?" thah high priest asked.

"Yeah." I broke tradition; Silence of thah Accused an' all that. Fuck it. I wasn't gonna let my own people burn me at thah stake without getting my two spells in. "First off, ma, I'm sohry. But it's true. They know it, I know it, it's whatevah. I'm a blood witch."

Again with thah shock an' horrah. It nevah got old. "So you're prob'ly gonna sentence me to death. A step outside thah law is a step outside of life. I learned that like all o' ya. Difference is, I only took of my life an' it was to save anothah. So this ain't no righteous act ya got goin' heah. It's murdah. If my death makes ya ask questions an' staht lookin' at things with less of a blind eye an' more of a third, then I ain't dyin' in vain. But heah is what I wanna let ya know, above all. What I did wasn't evil, and shouldn't be against any law whatsoevah."

Gasps filtahed through thah aih. I saw my ex-best friend covah her little brothah's eahs. I winked at him an' he smiled back. Maybe as long as he learned somethin' from this, I didn't die without purpose.

As thah talkin' hit a low roar stage, thah council erupted. "Enough!" thah high priest bellowed.

I smiled an' cast a futile wish for chewin' gum into thah ether. An' maybe a cigarette. That wouldn't suck. "Yeah, quiet down." I muttahed. "I gotta get to dyin'."

"Mia Redblade, kneel."

I walked out from behind my chaih an' stood before thah council. "I'll stand." I answahed. Thah high priest nodded and my mothah sobbed.

"For the crime of blood magic and the endangerment of your race in its practice, I, as High Priest of Red Coven, find you guilty and sentence you to death."

No shock this time, no gasps or whispahs. Not even that much grief. Soon, I'd be a page in a history book. But not without a final say.

"My blood will scream from thah ground." I promised. "An' thah powah will boil in your veins. I may be dyin, honey, but my death ends in revolution!"

"Shut up!" thah high priest lost his chill. "Choose now how you desire to die."

Not at all, you sunnavabitch.

I stayed quiet for a damn change; shook 'em up a bit. They stahted whispahrin' amongst themselves.

"Red Coven, hold your judgment." someone broke in. That voice wasn't a witch voice. Powah dripped from it like blood from a wound. I turned to stare.

Holy. Shit. Theah was a fuckin' angel in the courtroom.

"Your Eminence." thah high priest made an ass out of himself by bowin' an' scrapin', "as honored as we are by your presence, this is a trial."

"Hell no!" I broke in. "It's a pahty. Little tension, little gore, some teahs an' remorse. It's perfect!"

"Silence, witchling!" thah high priest bellowed. "You are nothing to us any longer! Mind your place!"

"Maybe nothing to you," thah angel spoke, entrancin' us to quiet once again. "But definitely of use to us. The Department of Angelic Affairs is recruiting. You don't want her; we will gladly take her off your hands."

Feah kicked in like a fuckin' mule. "Hell no. At least heah I know thah monstahs. I ain't sellin' my soul for a wing and a promise."

"Shut up, Redblade!" thah high priest ordahed. "Your Eminence, would you not care to choose from our more skilled, brighter young witches? We are certain that any of them would be willing to go with you."

Thah angel smiled, lullin' them into a stupah. "Your offer is generous, but we are not greedy. We will take your reject witch, and her alone. Rest assured, she will be punished for her crime, and molded to a brighter image."

I don't wanna go. Angels fuck ya up. Shit happens up theah that no one wants to talk about, even if they could. I think I'd rathah die.

Thah high priest sighed. "Mia Redblade, the coven rescinds your sentence, and turns you over to the Department of Angelic Affairs. Do your best not to disgrace us."

"I don't wanna go." I protested, knowin' they wouldn't care.

"Come with me, Mia." thah angel entreated. "We have such plans for you."

"I don't want nothin' to do with your goddamn depahtment."

"Quiet!" her voice lashed out in angelsong, an' my lips went numb. "Come. Now."

I walked forwahd, unwillin' to go but unable to resist. She might take me outtah heah, but no way in hell was I goin' to heaven.

Eternity Alone – Judah

The world is still turning. I can hear it, feel it, smell it. But I can do nothing about it. Centuries will teach you tolerance, but beyond that they are a school in apathy. When it is realized that change is the only constant, one begins to argue less and less until one does naught but sit back and watch.

And the heart longs for newness; for the intensity named desire—that sweet sweet tang of mortality. Funny, to still remember the taste of wine on my lips. To kill for it. No longer a crime of passion, but a crime of the memory of passion.

"The world unturns." I whispered, breathing against the window pane. It did not fog. "The cycle breaks. Kings and kingdoms climax and collapse. What new tragedy awaits, Darrintek?"

My friend, if one could call such a thing a friend, moved out from the shadows. "New turns, immortal, and cycles unspun. The world is shifting as kings are remade."

"You speak of distant dreams and revolution." I muttered, turning away from the frostbitten window.

"And you act like both are dead!" Tek exclaimed. "Are you so jaded, Judah? So immune to your own world? I tell you, heaven and hell are soon to be torn asunder."

"I want to believe you."

"Then believe!" he thundered. "You are chosen, Judah. Handpicked. For me, my friend, walk whatever road awaits you."

I tried to laugh, but the sound seemed harsh and grating, like the hinges of a rusty gate. "It's been so long, Darrin. The world is mine no longer."

"Stop with the morose vampire routine! It gets *old*! If you desire to keep up the cliché, smear yourself with glitter and fall in love with some stupid human girl who doesn't warrant your attention. Who knows, maybe if you do that you can taste the sun again."

Something, perchance even a flicker of true feeling, sparked in me. "After all these years...could it be?"

Darrintek smiled, never a sign of anything but promise. "There are loopholes within history, Judah. You only need find them to exploit them."

Lying violet eyes, I mused, finding the demon lovely for all of that. Time had not yet stolen my definition of beauty, only my appreciation of it.

"Loopholes within history." I repeated, anticipating the knock at my door.

It sounded and I answered it. A golden envelope was held out to me and I took it without a murmur. The material of the letter sang in my hands, echoes of symphonies my fingers had played...written.

"The Department of Angelic Affairs?" I asked, letting Darrintek see the return address.

He grinned, showing sharp, white teeth. "The world in chaos, little brother. Loopholes down rabbit holes."

"And if I comply with this insanity, then what?"

"Maybe you can find what you never could. What I could never, even in my power, procure. It's worth a shot, Judah."

"I dislike angels." I grumbled.

"As do I, but they have their uses. I suggest you find a way to turn their game in your favor."

I felt a rusty smile tug at the edges of my lips. To battle a worthy adversary, for the first time in centuries. I opened the letter and absorbed its contents.

"Well?" Tek asked.

"Apparently heaven is changing some rules." I replied, holding up a blood red, silver lined, embossed invitation. "I will be the first vampire given welcome there in four-hundred years."

"To the world's unturning." Tek raised an imaginary glass. He departed into the shadows, then back to his home...wherever that was.

I sank back into the comfortable leather of my chair. *Heaven*, I thought. *It's been a while.*

Moonlit Madness – Aislyn

Why, why, why tonight? I kept asking myself while I ran, focusing on the music blasting in my ears. The sun was up and I liked it there. It shouldn't ever change. The moon should never rise and never be full. I hated this time of the month more than the other one.

"Aislyn, get over here now!" my aunt yelled from the door.

I could have pretended that I didn't hear, but it would have been a lie. My hearing was too good for my own good. I took out my earphones and trotted up the steps. "Yes ma'am?"

"What in hell are you doing? Get yourself ready for the gathering."

I don't want to go! But I wouldn't dare say so out loud. I went upstairs to my room and jumped in the shower. After tonight I'd wake up naked and muddy, if I woke up at all. If I'd been wearing my fur, the ridge along my spine would be standing up.

I climbed out of the shower, trying to slow down my breathing. Just tonight. I could handle it tonight. Maybe.

"Aislyn!" the call beckoned me back down the stairs and into the car.

"Tonight is a big night." my aunt said as we pulled out of the driveway. "The alpha will be there."

"Oh." I wasn't interested. Unlike the rest of the pack, I despised our alpha. He was a son of a bitch. Literally. I laughed inside at my own horrible pun.

"Why?" I chose to keep the conversation going.

"This is one of the largest sections of the pack. He's concerned. There are things stirring in the underbelly of the earth. A gnawing and a twisting. Do you feel it at all?"

My stomach flipped. "All the time." I whispered, watching the setting sun. Already I could feel the moon beating down on me, demanding. I felt blood draining away from my face. It hurt. And the only one who felt such pain was me. Everyone else itched and scratched and waited for this one time per month. I dreaded it.

My aunt pulled the car into the parking lot and we walked to the Gather Point. The smell of the air was new; the same anticipation, tinted with an undercurrent of power that I hadn't felt before. All I felt was my own fear as the sun slipped below the horizon.

Cold sweat broke out on my forehead and my hands started shaking. Pain intensified, shooting through my bones. I bit back a gasp and walked behind my aunt, clenching my hands so they would stop shaking.

"Aislyn, are you all right?" she asked.

"Fine." I lied, trying to even out my breathing. *Just get this over with, please, please God.*

We entered the circle and sat down, waiting for the alpha to arrive. He did in short order, teeth gleaming like the sun, eyes an unholy shade of green.

"Welcome!" he boomed, and on cue, everyone bared their necks in submission. I didn't want to, or feel the need, but it was better in this place to remain quiet, humble, and unobserved.

Why today? I asked for the millionth time. *Why on this day, of all days?*

"We meet beneath the moon," the alpha began, "as brothers, sisters, and guardians. Pack. The world is darkening, turning in new cycles. We must take our place as leaders, wise-ones, and guides. With the moon, my people, rise to the darker side of beauty, and the curse that is our blessing!"

Eerie howls erupted, destroying the calm of the forest. It was true that we were guardians, an ancient clan of warriors who failed in their duties and were cursed by long-dead human magic to forever protect humanity. But it was still a curse…I would never see this as a blessing. Never.

I crept into a shadowed crevice, shaking with pain. Letting tears fall, I surrendered my soul to the moon. Agony wracked every joint, every nerve. Acid ran through my veins, scouring away my skin, my bones, the shape of the body I knew as mine. Waves of black swarmed over my eyes and choked off my breath, taking me to places darker than dreams. Memory...

...excitement...rush...newness. the moon gleams through the windows, full and bright with promise. I run into the room, dancing for joy, then freeze. Smell of Fear. confusion. a little girl stumbles into a room and there's blood and there's red and mom and dad aren't mom and dad anymore but lifeless shells with glowing golden eyes and the room smells like hot metal and the girl is not a girl anymore but a wolf who jumps on the men who smell like leather and silver and tears out their throats...and realization that killers are human and humans off limits to the jaws of the werewolf...no one can know that the moon is a killer, but blood has its memories, it stains and it lingers, reminding, reminding, reminding, reminding...

...a horrid, keening wail shrieked through the trees, ripped from my voice. Rain beat down; my naked body shivered. The smell of blood washed over me, sweet and sickening. "No." I whispered. "I don't want to be this. I don't want to remember..." *how I killed them.*

"Then do not." a glowing hand appeared before my swimming vision. "I can take your pain away. All of it."

I looked into the face of the person who owned the hand. Beautiful brown eyes reached into my soul and warmed it. "Who are you?" I asked.

"A guardian of guardians." came the answer. "A protector. You fear this place, you fear your memory, and the punishment they would surely pronounce for a crime you did not commit. Come with me. I will keep you safe. I promise."

The guarantee of safety comforted me beyond degree. It was something I had never been offered. "Where will we go?" I asked.

"Heaven." she whispered. "I will take you into heaven."

"Am I dying?" I asked, afraid.

"No. You are chosen. Take my hand."

I reached for her hand, feeling fear evaporate at her touch. The world flashed white.

Vows Forsaken – Kieran

I parked the car in front of my mother's house. We unloaded all the stuff she didn't need and couldn't live without. I smiled as the familiar scents of home greeted me. But I didn't live here anymore. I'd left after...after my recovery. It was best to have my nightmares alone. I didn't like to worry my mother. She had my brothers and sisters to care for. I couldn't be that selfish, even though I wanted to be...sometimes. I did enjoy freedom from the incessant hovering.

"Children!" my mom called. "Come help me and your sister!"

A chorus of voices followed and I found myself swarmed by those delightful creatures known as younger siblings. They gave me quick hugs and dashed out to the car.

"Where's Reya?" I asked about my younger sister. She was two years younger than I, and we were as close as two sisters could be.

"I'm right here." said the voice that had nursed me through fever dreams and gaping wounds. My sister gave me a hug and kissed the scar on my cheek. "Are you all right?" she asked, still careful to avoid touching me where she might hurt me. It seemed that no one would believe I had healed.

"I'm fine." I answered, smiling for her comfort and mine.

"Ready for your wedding?" she needled.

"No." I grinned; softened. "I'm not ready."

Our mother left the room and Reya scrutinized me. "I understand." she sighed. "You're not ready, and honestly, I don't think they've told him about...what you've been through."

What you've been through...like torture and its effects are something easily explained. "You can't know unless you've been there. But...tradition."

"Oh, fuck tradition!" Reya exclaimed, shocking me. "All it does is screw up our lives. You've broken it once before, when you joined our armies."

"And look at the price I've paid for that. Mother hates what happened but I know she's relieved that I'm too broken to fight anymore."

"Only your body is broken." Reya reminded me, fierce. "Your will and your mind are intact. Please, sis, for those of us who aren't strong enough to."

I smiled and hugged my sister again. I owed her my life...and much more than that. "You can do anything." I promised her. "Even defy elven tradition."

"But it's easier when you do it." she laughed.

I joined in until a familiar scent sent shockwaves of horror down my spine. "Reya, does it smell like cinnamon to you?"

She sniffed the air. "Yeah, now that you mention it. But we haven't been cooking anything with cinnamon..."

I ran to the window. "Mom, get the kids in the house!" I yelled, feeling the familiar burn of adrenaline. I turned to Reya. "Take care of them; make sure you have an exit. No basement, no attic. Don't do *anything* until I come back."

"Kieran, what's going on?" Mother asked as she and the kids poured into the room. "Why does it smell like cinnamon?"

I swallowed, trying to control my fear. "Witch magic...smells like cinnamon." *So it's pleasant when you die.*

"Kieran, no!" mom shrieked, but I was out of the door.

I ran, feeling my lungs protest, but I shoved regrets out of my mind. My body was broken. Broken by witches. If they were after me, they were dead. If they wanted my family, I would throw them into hell.

The cinnamon smell became overwhelming as I turned a corner. A solitary witch battled creatures in black leather.

Those aren't elves, I realized. They were something much darker. And the witch was trying to kill them. *The enemy of my enemy is...not yet my enemy.*

I reached into my boot and pulled out my silver dagger. I threw it, hoping my time with the witches had not erased all my skills. The blade struck true and one of the black leather monsters fell, screaming in a language I'd never heard before.

I ran to the aid of the witch, who was busy having her defensive circle pummeled by three of the...whatever they were. I pulled my knife from the now smoking corpse of the creature and hurried over to the witch.

The edges of her shield swept out; one of the tendrils sliced open my arm. The creatures, with their shiny violet eyes and red, scaly skin, caught the scent of blood and turned to me. I jumped back as one lashed out, barely evading the taloned hand that could tear me to pieces. I ducked and leapt out, sliding my knife into its chest, twisting as hard as I could, and pulling the blade up and out. The monster hacked and screamed, but fell and began to smoke.

A fist rammed into my back and I coughed as pain ricocheted through my bones. I turned and sliced the blade across my attacker's throat. Another strangled scream, and smoke instead of blood. I tried to regain bearing as I caught my balance. There had been four...where was the last?

I tuned my ears, as vision had been rendered useless by the smoke bleeding from the bodies. Noise...I spun in time to face the bladed claws headed for my throat. A million thoughts flashed through me, regret, anger, love...all shattered by a bolt of red lightning. Smoke billowed into the air and the creature, or rather parts of it, splattered on the ground.

"Thank the Goddess." I breathed.

The curtain of smoke moved and a boot planted itself in my ribs, knocking me back. I gasped for air as the wind flew out of me, remembering a none too distant agony. A hand smelling of cinnamon held a knife to my throat.

"Get off me, witch!" I sputtered, furious. "I just saved your life!"

To my shock, the knife moved, and the hand helped me to my feet. Snapping blue eyes glared at me, filled with distrust and exhaustion.

"I don't want to harm you." I said, calm. "Are you all right?"

The eyes blinked, dazed. She was white as a sheet. "Just fuckin' ducky." a trickle of blood slipped from her nose over her lips. "I think...maybe...I ovahdid it a little."

She swayed and I caught her before she fell. "Why did you attack me?" I asked.

Sleepy, beautiful blue eyes struggled to focus. "I'm runnin' from thah angels. You kindah looked like one."

Shock struck me as the witch's eyes rolled back in her head and she lost consciousness. I lifted her, ignoring twin pains from my arm and my ribs, and slung her over my shoulder. She weighed almost nothing at all.

Why the hell is a witch running from angels? I wondered. *And why is she in elven territory? Even with the treaty, witches know better than to cross this side of the lines. What in hell is going on?*

I approached my mother's house and opened the passenger door of my car. Then, careful, I eased the witch into the seat. Her eyes had purple shadows under them from exhaustion. I couldn't help but feel pity.

"Kieran." my mother ran from the front door down to my side. "Are you all right? Are you hurt? Are the witches gone?"

"I'm fine." I tried to wipe the pain from my eyes so she wouldn't see. "The witch wasn't attacking. She was being attacked. I saved her."

"You what!?" Reya shrieked, grabbing my wounded arm. I hissed in pain and they saw the blood. "Kieran, you're hurt." my younger sister breathed. "Come inside. Let me take care of you."

"I can't." I answered, feeling sorrow. They would never understand. I could not ask them to. "I have to help her."

My mother spat in the direction of the passenger seat. "Damn her and her kind. Come inside, Kieran."

I remembered the red lightning. "She saved my life." I told them, removing my arm from Reya's grasp. "I owe her something."

"If anyone has a reason to hate witches, it's you, Kieran." she reminded me. "They've taken everything from you."

I smiled and opened the driver's door. "That's why I have to change something." I said, shutting the door. *Hopefully everything. Hopefully the world.*

I turned the key and backed out of the driveway. On the way home, I looked at the unconscious witch in my car.

I'm runnin' from thah angels. You kindah looked like one.

I am watching you, my new Messiah. Traditions are sundered, ancient hates forgotten. All I see is the potential for greatness.

You are a traitor in every way. My beautiful revolutionary. When will the time be right? When will you come to me? I cannot force you, but if you only knew how I have waited for you, if you knew mine was the voice that brought you out from hell.

Plans are in motion, my darling, plans to alter the Fate Path of History. The Eyes of Eternity are yours, if you will take them. I will offer you the world, only hear, only understand. Everything I do is for you. Please, forgive me.

"Mother, I swear, if you ask if I'm all right one more time, I will hurt someone. And it won't be the witch."

I watched thah woman pace thah floor, grittin' her teeth an' lookin' like a panthah in a cage.

"Mom, I know what I'm doing. Just...trust me, all right? Yes, I cleaned it. Yes, it stopped bleeding. I'm going to hang up now. Don't call back. I promise I'm okay. Bye, mom."

I sat up an' thah room stahted spinnin'. "Aw, fuck me." I groaned, floppin' back down on thah couch. My bones ached an' my head hurt like a fuckin' fury.

"You're awake." she had a cultured voice, cool and serene. I didn't hate it. "How do you feel?"

"Like a Mack truck smacked me between thah eyes." I tried to reach my powah centah, hit nothin'. "Fuck, that's why. I'm tapped out." I tried sittin' up again, watchin' everythin' tilt like a rollah coastah.

"Lie back." she said, an' cool hands eased my shouldahs down. "I've seen witches who use too much power. You have to be careful."

"Right. Fuckin' sorcerah's curse." I opened my eyes an' focused on her face. Full lips, thin nose, slight jaw. Eyes blackah than death's hand raked ovah me. An' her eahs were pointy. Realization honked its ugly-ass horn.

"Holy shit, you're an elf!" I exclaimed, wishin' I felt strong enough to run for my life.

This was mega-level not good. Elves didn't like witches...mostly 'cause we destroyed almost all of them duhrin' thah countless wars we'd fought. An' witches weren't kind to enemies. I'd learned that first hand.

"My name is Kieran." I didn't know whethah or not that voice soothed me or freaked me out now. "You were being attacked. I came to help you. Do you remember me?"

"Since when does an elf help a witch?" I asked. If she'd been elven to thah core, I'd be dead along with whatevah it was that attacked me.

"I didn't like those things near my family. You were fighting them. Enemy of my enemy..."

"But you're an elf."

"I believe we've already stated the obvious." she grinned.

"You okay?" I asked, stahtin' to feel sleepy again.

"I'm more worried about you at the moment."

"Pretty eyes." I shivahed as my eyes closed. "Pretty eyes shouldn't be so worried."

"Go to sleep." her cool hand eased my eyes closed.

∞

Thah sun was settin' when I woke up thah next time. I kept quiet, watchin' my elven hostess. I still didn't trust her, mostly 'cause I knew wheah she got that scar on her face. No elf with that would treat a witch right. I knew I sure as hell wouldn't.

She lifted her shirt, exposin' thah purple an' green mess of her ribs. I winced. I'd done that to her, an' it looked like it hurt. She touched the bruises, doubled ovah, an' hissed. Ah, shit. I'd prob'ly fucked her up. But I'd thought she was an angel. An' they'd been some saintly pissed off mothah fuckers.

"Hey, gal, you all right?" I asked, hatin' than I felt worse.

Soft laughtah from thah cornah. "I think you cracked some bones." she joked. "I'll be fine. Are you feeling any better?"

"Nah." my honesty suhprised me. Then I remembahed. It's tough to lie to an elf. That's why their interrogations were a lot less brutal an' lots more efficient. "I feel all hollow an' lost. It's freakin' me out."

She rose from her seat an' knelt by thah couch. I could tell thah movement hurt her. Brave little elf. "You're separated." she mumbled, feelin' my forehead. God, her hands were soft. "It's a witch thing. When you're tapped out, you lose spiritual connection and focus. It jacks you around inside until it equalizes on some plane."

"I know." I reached out an' touched her scar with my fingahtips. "How long did they have you?" I asked.

Her eyes flashed to mine, angry. "What?"

My vision was fuzzin' out again. "I know." I whispahed. "I know what they did to ya. I'm sohry."

She took my hand away. "What's your name?" she asked.

"Mia. Mia Redblade."

She said somethin' else, but thah words were all fuzzy and distohted. God, this passin' out bit was gettin' old.

You're leaving me, aren't you? Leaving me before I can show you my love and the truth. One tender touch dissuades you from the Way?

Why choice and choosing? Why burning flames and cinnamon oil to scent and heat the night? The scroll of your life is before me, and pain reaches out from the words.

The ink of your life is smeared with my blood. I have edited this at the cost of my hope. But I do not need the hope I have given. I have you. You return to me everything I have lost.

It is within my power. It is within my rights. I am willing to sacrifice the world for you. I am willing…and unable. But you can make me able. Give me the one thing greater than hope. Love me…

"I trust you will be comfortable here." my guide said, opening the door.

I walked into a room where the air felt clean, not just smelled it. White carpet, softer than down feathers, covered the floors and walls. Windows looked out on gleaming buildings set on foundations of clouds. There were animals flying that I'd never seen before, lions with wings and breathing creatures made of glass.

The streets I could see from the windows gleamed gold and the sun was silver. I turned to face the smile of my guide. "Is this really mine?" I asked.

"Of course." his smile widened. "This is your home now."

"And the sun never sets?" hope sprang up in my heart. No moon. No curse. I would be free from it at last.

"Never. This is the Land of Endless Day." he assured me. "It's hard to believe, I know. But you are safe now."

"Why just me?" the question I'd been too afraid to ask slipped out. "Why not anyone else?"

"Because no one else has what you have, my girl. However, that can wait. Once you've settled in, we'll go see the Secretary."

"Secretary of what?" I asked another question. Curiosity killed the cat, not the wolf.

"The Department of Angelic Affairs. The governing body of Heaven."

I swallowed, hard. He had just told me I was going to see the President of Heaven. "Okay." my voice sounded small. "Will you come and get me? I don't want to be late."

"All is taken care of." he walked to me and cupped my cheek. "You shouldn't look so worried, Aislyn. This is Heaven. Fear nothing. We will take care of you."

Comfort enveloped me as he left the room. I wondered about my aunt and the rest of the pack. They probably didn't miss me. For a moment, I missed them. But they weren't my life anymore. This was, and I would do anything for the angels.

No one cared about the werewolves, not the elves, not the witches, not the vampires. Definitely not the vampires. So far the only ones to show the wolves compassion were the angels.

I shivered as a new thought entered my mind. Nothing came for free, least of all paradise. What would my saviors charge for my salvation?

Demon in Paradise – Judah

Nothing changes in heaven. Funny, that the arbiters of change keep themselves at a level constant. But that is history, repetitive hypocrisy and attempts for the majority vote. Circles within circles and worlds within worlds.

"Am I doomed to wait here forever?" I asked. "Trust me, I will. I have that much time."

"What right does a damned one have to challenge Heaven's gates?" a voice boomed.

I laughed at the theatrics. Then I retrieved the invitation. "I'm not challenging heaven, love. I'm welcome here."

A short angel came to the gate and examined my invitation, then looked at me with keen eyes. "It seems legitimate. What a record breaking day. Come in. You have a meeting with the Secretary. Keep it quiet and maybe we can get you out of here without a fuss."

I chuckled to myself as I entered the gates. A record breaking moment and the angels were keeping it quiet. Nothing must change in heaven. No one must know of the holes in the armor of Paradise.

The tiny angel led me through the back alleyways of heaven, darting into side-streets and climbing on top of buildings. I followed, fighting the urge to laugh. Even the smallest, youngest angel could kill me. But they feared us, the soulless bastard children of their willful ways.

"This is entirely unnecessary." I told him as we walked through even more labyrinthine alleyways. "I'm not here to cause trouble."

"Look," his tone grew snarky, "I don't know what the Secretary is doing, but I don't agree with letting vampires into Heaven. What I do know is that plans are in motion to shake the world at its core. I assume your presence here has something to do with that."

I dislike being used. I thought, following the angel into a small side door. I bristled, watching the flurry of activity and hearing nothing but silence. I was accustomed to human chaos, mortal machines and voices echoing. But angels could speak mind to mind, keeping chaos internal.

Strange little world, I mused, again following my stature-deprived guide. He led me to a room of simple elegance, where the chair seemed as though it played music. My instincts riled. I was a vampire, a warrior, an immortal. I would not be seduced and taken down by Heaven's manipulations.

"I do not like this." I stated, refusing to sit in the musical chair.

"Feel free to stand." my guide smiled. "The Secretary will be with you shortly. In the mean time, may I offer you something...no. I don't supposed you'd like anything to drink."

I tried to smile, but was not up the task. He had said that with purpose. Drinking angel's blood was akin to drinking sunlight. It would kill the presumptuous vampire who touched it to their lips. None could drink the blood of angels but demons. It was their right, after all. They were the only race powerful enough to kill an angel.

"I will be fine." I told my guide. "You've no need to hover."

"Very well." he answered, eager to leave the room. "As I said, the Secretary will arrive soon."

"I wait with bated, non-existent, breath."

Ah, sweet silence. Tranquil, tranquil, peace and quiet. You're waiting, my wounded warrior. Waiting for your redemption, for your salvation. We are not so different, you and I.

Do you feel the same longing, an ache that twists your sleep into bracelets of thorns? Do you long as I long, to hold what you have never possessed, and keep it safe for longer than eternity? I know that you do. We are not so unalike, you and I.

So I ask you now, a far greater task than any I have commissioned in my long years. Find the missing piece, the one who calls to both of us with the symphony of the sun. Find it, my love, and save us all.

Fleeing Heaven – Kieran

The clock on the oven flipped from 11:59 to midnight. The witching hour. I looked at the witch asleep on my couch. Her condition had gone from not good to worse. Witches were like elves, connected to the world within the world, the various spiritual planes.

To lose connection to those planes, even temporarily, was dangerous and painful. To be stripped from it forever was...hell.

I moved from my chair, wincing as my body protested. The cut on my arm was deep; deep enough to need stitches. I would have to do without. Another scar wouldn't kill me, even if it was ugly. I sat down by the witch, listening to her uneven breathing.

Why? I asked. *Why did I do that? Why did I save her? And why, why in the Goddess' name, is she on the run from angels?*

My eyes flitted to the gold satin envelope on my table, next to the white garment bag. I didn't know what I feared the contents of more. I rose and grabbed the envelope; returned to my seat and stared at it.

TO KIERAN SHANDERA: FROM THE DEPARTMENT OF ANGELIC AFFAIRS

What did they want? With me or the witch?

I tore the edge of the envelope and the witch's, Mia's, eyes flashed open. "Don't." she whispered, voice raspy.

"Don't what?" I asked, grateful she was awake.

"Open it." her blue eyes glimmered fever-bright. "You'll regret it. And you're...a good person. Don't let them take you."

Her voice became frantic and I tried to calm her. "Shhh. Don't talk. You have to save your strength. You need rest, Mia."

I smoothed her hair back as her eyes closed, feeling the heat radiating from her skin. I hoped this was as bad as it would get, for her sake. It could be much worse.

She jerked in her sleep. "You...know my name. Why...did they do...what they did...to you?"

"I don't know." I whispered, wiping her brow with a cool washcloth. Tears pricked and two fell. I didn't bother to wipe them away. "I just don't know."

Ignoring the pain, present and past, I withdrew the contents of the letter. The paper felt solid and smooth in my hand, almost like glass.

To Kieran Shandera, Elf:
The Secretary of Angelic Affairs desires to meet with you as soon as possible. It is a matter of grave importance and concerns not only you, but the entire elven race. Urgency is needed. When you decide to answer this invitation, we will know, and a way into Heaven will be provided for you. Please decide as soon as possible. We cannot stress the importance of this.
With all Respect:
The Department of Angelic Affairs

"Urgent matter?" I asked the silence of my apartment. "They will know when I've made my decision?" I glanced at the witch on my couch. "Am I being...watched?"

"K...Kieran." Mia was sitting up, breathing heavy, staring at me with heated eyes. "You gotta go...they, they know you opened thah lettah. Go...I'll...take care of it."

Fear struck through me. She wasn't lying. It was difficult to lie to an elf. "I'm not leaving you here." I rose and gasped at the twinge of pain. "You're sick."

"I'll only," she swung her legs over the edge of the couch, "slow ya down. You've helped me enough."

"No." I emphasized the world. Then I started throwing things together. "I won't let them take you."

I finished packing and flung my bag across my shoulders. I didn't need much to survive, and, due to my soldier's training, little time to prepare.

I sat down beside the witch, hoisting her arm over my shoulders. "Lean on me." I directed, standing up.

"Why..." her head dropped, "...ah you helpin' me?"

"Because if they catch you, you will be a prisoner." I ground out as we walked to the door. "And I don't know how angels treat their prisoners."

Her soft, pained whimper made me stop. "Bettah than witches do...I think."

"Let's not find out." I started moving again, almost dragging Mia with me.

We made it down the stairs and out of the apartments. Again, I found myself helping the witch into the passenger side of my car. Once she was situated, I dashed to the driver's side and climbed in. The car roared to life when I turned the key and I threw it in gear, pulling out of my driveway as another vehicle pulled in...one unfamiliar to the complex.

I kept driving, afraid to look back in case I was being followed. I stared at the passed-out witch in my car.

This just gets better and better.

Predator and Prey – Judah

Angels do not see time. It has no bearing on their lives, little effect on their Fate Path. What will happen, will happen in its own time. Thus it follows that they keep to no schedule of promise in time.

I waited in the room, listening to the soothing strains of the musical chair.

"How long must I linger in heaven?"

The door opened and radiance entered the room. I rose in respect and awe, touched for the first time by light that did not burn me. The luminosity dimmed and my eyes took in what I would wager could be Heaven's most beautiful angel.

Her silver eyes gleamed and scarlet hair fell nearly to the floor. Razor sharp features seemed somehow gentle when generous lips curved in a smile.

"Welcome." her voice sounded like waterfalls and earthquakes. "I am the Secretary of Angelic Affairs. You may call me Josephine."

I regained composure. "A pleasure to meet you, Madame Secretary. I would introduce myself, but I believe you know everything already."

She laughed. To my surprise, it seemed genuine. "I do, and that only makes this simpler. We can give you what you most desire. We know you have tried...alternative alliances...to procure it."

"Angelic blackmail?" I asked. "I thought Heaven rose above such human means. Am I mistaken?"

"There are certain limitations in Heaven." Josephine continued, disregarding my question. "And so we have to contract out. There are two who have defied Heaven's law. We need them brought in as soon as possible. One is a blood witch who escaped from our custody. Another is an elf who is aiding her escape."

I snickered. "One lone witch breaks out of heaven? Whatever happened to your security?"

The Secretary looked offended. "She had to use all her magic, so we know she's not in the best of health. But we do not want her to die. She is a heavenly asset. The elf aiding her was sent an invitation much akin to yours. While their meeting is coincidence, their alliance is unprecedented and problematic. The elf is a warrior. This is why we are endeavoring to contract you."

"*If* I agree." I hastened to say, though I could not deny that the story tempted me.

Elves and witches hated each other, more than angels and demons. That one would help the other was...a ridiculous notion. A radical change.

"We hope you will." Josephine said. "We need a hunter, which is why we were hoping to come to an agreement with you. Of course you will not be alone. We have another who has agreed to do this for us."

"And all you want me to do is bring in a witch and an elf?"

"Yes."

"And you will return to me what was stolen?"

"Of course. We have the requisition paperwork going up the chain now. I can personally guarantee it will go through."

Dreams, elusive things to torment the mind, to keep alive the beautiful human fallacy of hope. It should be wrong for us, less or more than human, to have dreams, cling to them, steal hope from the world. But we do.

"I will do it." I said, remembering Darrintek's advice. "Who am I working with?"

The Secretary smiled, spilling light into the room. "Thank you. You have Heaven's gratitude. Your companion is here now."

The door opened and a slight, pretty redhead entered. Amber eyes looked at me and a primal growl echoed through the room. I turned to Josephine.

"No one told me I'd be working with a mutt."

"Reya, calm down." thah elf's voice again. "I'll be fine. Something came up and I had to leave."

Silence.

"No...no. I don't know when I'll be back. Guess this means the wedding's off? I'll try not to be heart-broken. Take care of mom for me. Let her know I'm all right. I have to go. I love you, sis."

I sat up an' it made me feel breathless, but at least thah world wasn't spinnin' like a tilt-a-whirl. This wasn't thah room I'd woke up in thah first time.

"Wheah thah hell ah we?"

"Safe, for now." my elf answahed. "How do you feel?"

"Like I just went through thah spin cycle. All wrung out."

"Makes sense." she sat down, winced. "Your fever broke last night."

"How much fuckin' time have I lost?" I wondahed, hatin' how confused I was.

"Probably a day and a half." she glanced at thah clock. "You haven't been in the best of shape. I'm sorry I wasn't able to do more for you."

I still didn't trust her, but she seemed honest enough. An' she'd saved my life. My own people didn't do that. They fuckin' let me go with thah celestial butchas.

"I owe ya a lot." I said, hidin' my face from those wicked, spahkin' black eyes.

"I would just like to know what I'm running from. I've never been in this situation before. The angels have left the elves very much alone. Can you at least tell me what in hell is happening?"

I sighed. She desehved an explanation. "Long story short, I'm not ya normal witch. I use...blood magic."

She just nodded. That suhprised me. Most elves tripped out about blood magic, what with it bein' stereotypically evil an' shit.

"Go on."

"So, my coven doesn't really like it. They don't really like it a lot. So they sorta sentenced me to death."

"They're merciful to their own." Kieran muttahed, lookin' anywheah but at me.

I sobahed as I realized she was right. Witches were good at torturin'. They sucked at mercy an' compassion. Then again, so did every race.

"Yeah, a cruel sorta kindness. Anyhow, they're about to tell me how I'm gonna die when an angels busts up in theah an' bahgains for my life. The coven don't give a shit an' they sell me off. Just less papahwork for them to do."

"Witches have paperwork for executions?" she almost laughed.

"Yeah. If it's legal it leaves a papah trail. Gotta love it. Anyhow, thah angels lock me in a fuckin' tiny room an' staht throwin' all these tests at me. An' not tests like IQ or inkblot shit eithah. They fuckin' ripped inside my head and tried to figuah out what made me tick. They tried to shred my soul. Maybe even got a piece. That's what they're fuckin'

38

with up theah. Some sorta freaktastic experiment with souls."

"What sort of experiments?" she asked, lookin' thoughtful.

"Don't know. Aftah I recovahed from them pokin' around in theah, I broke out. I guess it did a numbah on me. Weren't for you, I'd be dead. Or worse."

"My pleasure." thah words actually sounded real, like she meant 'em. "I'm sorry you had to go through that."

Yeah, but—I could get away. You don't escape from witches. An' angels ahn't as cruel.

"It's all right." I felt subdued, not a place I often stood. "So, you're a soldiah?"

"Was." her voice took a dahk tone. "I was a captive when the war ended. As part of the treaty, both sides returned all prisoners. I was one of them, and they left me, almost dead, in front of my mother's house. When I healed, I was too broken to re-enter the service." A grim smile quirked her lips. "Honorable discharge."

"Fuck." I said thah first thing that came to mind. "An' now you're stuck with ya worst enemy on thah run from Heaven."

Anothah smile. I decided I liked it. "I knew I'd never have an easy life. And you're not my worst enemy, Mia."

Thah sohrow in her tone convinced me it was true.

"Then what am I? 'Cause I know damn well any witch who had done to them what you had done to you would be lookin' to kill any elf they could get their hands on."

Kieran's black eyes went somewheah even darkah. "And what changes then? We keep on killing for vengeance and our children die for nothing."

I chuckled. She sounded like a fuckin' tree huggin' idealist. "So you wanna die for somethin'?"

"Hell no!" she exclaimed, stahtlin' me. "I want to live for something."

Thah beauty of that struck a chord in me, of things I longed for. I looked at thah elf and opened my mouth to continue thah convahsation when thah door exploded intah splintahs.

This is not at all what I had planned. I am no lover of chaos. I hoped you would come to me, as you have, but more...willing. Why are there dark corners in your heart, pockets and shadows and mysteries to be unraveled? Why are you allowed choices that bring you pain; that make you bleed?

I want to hold you in my arms and sing for you eternity. It is a song of beautiful things forgotten, of treasures lost and locked in time. It is my song, dearest one, a song I pray I can rewrite. But someone's blood must ink the lyrics, and I have never known a wound. Tell me, my Messiah, what is it to feel power ebbing from your body?

What is it to die for what you love?

Partners… – Aislyn

My hackles went up when I walked into the room and saw a vampire. I cursed at myself for not smelling him first. What didn't help was the fact that he was hot…really hot.

Hazel eyes with a whole lot of green, mocha skin and coffee colored hair that that hung in smooth waves to his shoulders.

"I'm not a mutt." I defended myself.

The Secretary, Josephine, looked at us both so sharply I was tempted to check for bleeding.

"Aislyn is a werewolf from a…different background. We think she might be of some help in your search. Her senses are nearly as keen and…well…she can walk in daylight."

The vampire grunted and Josephine looked at me again.

"Madame Secretary, forgive me, but do you truly intend to send me against a blood witch and an elven warrior with this…child?"

I wanted to speak up, take my side, but I figured it was better to let Josephine do the talking.

"Aislyn is older than you think. Are you so old and jaded that you give the young no chances? Remember, master vampire, I am a good deal older than even you. Will you have it said that you disagreed with angels?"

The vamp frowned, sending lines deep into his skin. "No." he muttered.

"Then I will leave the two of you to become acquainted. Aislyn, meet Judah. And both of you, remember, you are no longer simply vampire and werewolf. You have been contracted by Heaven to perform a vital and dangerous task."

Josephine left the room…leaving me alone with the leech.

"Do you know how much I have riding on this, little mutt?" he asked, raking me over with eyes that flashed yellow, much like my own.

"Probably as much as I do." I growled. "You think you're the only one with something riding on this deal?"

He looked offended for a moment. "Well."

"Look," I laid it out straight, "I'm not exactly thrilled about working with a leech."

"Ha!" he laughed, then stopped, surprised. "You've got spunk, mutt. I can work with that."

"You better." I said. "'Cause I'm not about to be left behind."

"Very well then. Let's get out of Heaven, shall we?"

I nodded, but I let him walk out of the room ahead of me.

Worst Case Scenario – Kieran

I stood up and clutched the knife in my boot. Mia rolled from the couch and under the coffee table.

"Fuck!" she yelled. "Damn angels!"

I stared at the creature that had torn down the door. Light radiated from the golden sword it held, and the face of a lioness on the body of a human snarled at me. Indigo wings cramped in the small room and feathers fell from them.

"Kieran Shandera and Mia Redblade, you are bound by the law of Heaven. Stand down."

Fear, real and true, sizzled through my veins like lightning. I would not be taken again. Neither god nor angels would hold me prisoner.

"Tell whoever sent you to fuck themselves." I said, watching the angel's teeth ripple back.

"This is your final warning. Stand. Down."

I glanced to make sure Mia was safe. Then I looked at the seraphim. "No."

The golden blade swept out for my neck. I ducked under it and charged in, trying to make the length of his sword ineffectual. His hand jerked up and his fist caught under my jaw. My head snapped back and I saw dark spots. But he was not going to drag me anywhere I did not want to go.

"Son of a bitch!" I cursed, climbing to my feet.

My knife still felt solid in my hand. The angel's eyes flickered. Again the golden blade snapped out. I dodged and dashed in close once more. My blade scored his arm and he yowled in pain. I laughed, loving the adrenaline.

This, I thought, *this is why I did what I did. Why I became a warrior. To protect.*

I flipped my blade over and prepared to drive it into the angel's heart. It wouldn't kill it. You could never *kill* angels.

The seraph dropped his sword and his hands closed around my throat. Fire locked behind my eyes and I struggled for air. The grip tightened and black flashed in front of my eyes.

"Get ya filthy hands off her!" I heard a yell...very far away.

The vice around my neck dropped and I fell to the floor, coughing as I sucked down air. When my vision cleared, I looked up. The seraph clawed at two glowing crimson hands across his throat. I glanced over to see the witch on her knees, bleeding from two shallow cuts on her arms.

I scooped up my knife from the ground and stood. "Break the spell!" I yelled not wanting her to over-extend herself.

The crimson light cords dropped and I rammed my blade into the angel's chest. Blue blood fountained out; I screamed as it burned my skin.

The angel clutched at the wound, staring at me with confusion in his glittering predator's eyes. "How?"

Bewildered, I watched as the creature sank to the floor, as his eyes closed, and as his chest ceased to rise and fall.

I just...did that...did I truly...

"Holy shit!" Mia exclaimed.

I turned to look at her, seeing fear in her eyes.

"You...you just killed an angel!"

I ran to the sink and washed the angel's burning blood from my hands. Mia followed me. She was pale, frighteningly so.

"Are you all right?" I asked.

"Ah you?" she snapped. "I just watched ya do thah impossible. I'm a little freaked."

"Me too." I breathed, looking at the cuts on her forearms.

I did not know much about blood magic, but it looked like she'd be all right.

45

"Whadda we do?"

"It's not like we can hide here." I said, a horrible plan forming in my head. "They've already proven that they can find us."

"So wheah do we go?" she wondered. "Killin' an angel...do they even have a sentence for that?"

"We can't risk finding out." I left the room and grabbed my bag. "So we have to go to a place where killing an angel is not a crime."

"Aw, fuck me." she groaned. "We're goin' to hell, ahn't we?"

Hunting – Judah

The door of the room did not exist. If it did, it was the sawdust on the floor. The mutt and I exchanged glances.

"Smells like blood." we spoke in unison.

I grunted and crossed the threshold. The room was in disarray, tables turned over, drops of blood staining the carpet.

"Oh...my...god." the mutt breathed, dropping to her knees.

I turned and felt my face deepen into a frown. "Is that..."

"It's an angel." she whispered. "And he's dead."

Angels did not die. Vampires and elves were immortal in the sense that they would live forever unless their lives were ended by force. With angels and demons it was different. Only one thing could kill them, and it was not witch magic or elven steel.

"Do you think?" she asked, sensing the pattern of my thoughts.

"No. They are not working with demons. You'd be able to smell the sulfur. And what do you sense?"

She sniffed the air, analyzing it. "Blood." she answered. "Blood and steel, magic and fear. But no sulfur."

"Hence my concern." I sharpened my vision in the dark.

I saw only angel feathers and drops of the witch's blood. The sole sign of the elf was the faint scent of sunlight in their steel. While we were not natural enemies, elven blood was exquisite and rare, as only another immortal's can be. They had learned to defend themselves, as elven blood, unlike that of angels, would not kill us.

"So, where do you think they went?"

"Silence, mutt. I am thinking."

"Well think out loud. We're working together, you know."

"I do not think so well out loud and...why am I arguing with you. Shut up."

She glared at me. "That was uncalled for."

"Perhaps, but you're wasting time. Just be silent for a few moments."

"Fine." she growled, leaving me to examine the body of the angel once more.

What is possessing them to do this? I wondered. *It goes beyond logic and reason. No sane man defies heaven or hell. But here are these two, killing angels...somehow. They have no refuge left on this earth.*

"Which is why they are not here." I muttered, realizing.

"They're in hell." the mutt broke in.

"How do you figure?" I asked, grudgingly impressed.

"I followed the smell of the angel's blood out into the hall."

"Yes?"

"The scent vanished, replaced by the scent of sulfur."

"But there are no gates near here. I would sense them."

Confusion entered her eyes. "Which means?"

"Which means someone must have opened the door for them. It does not shock me...however this angel died, hell would be aware of its passing."

"Would a demon do that?" she inquired.

"Some. One I know in particular." I looked at her, so young, fighting against those who had battled for centuries. "Come, mutt."

"Where are we going?"

"Hell, my dear." I flashed a devilish smile.

She half-laughed as we left the room. "You sure know how to romance a girl...for a leech."

Where are they going, straying from my sight? I never meant for this, and now there is blood. The scent of it chokes me, brings tears to my eyes. I never intended for this to enter the world below.

All have gone, and you with them, my precious Messiah. Why do you think you will find what you seek from your enemy? They will lie to you, my love, deceive you and hang you from the city gates.

The Way has been made clear to you, my darling. Why do you refuse to walk the easy path? I am still longing for you, my dearest one. The world is yours. Only ask. Only return.

Fuckin' Angels Man — Mia

"Please, feel at ease." our host said, smilin'.

Violet eyes gleamed an' I felt a tad uneasy. We were in hell. We were in hell with a demon who was bein' nice as pie.

"Fohgive me if I'm a little untrustin'." I said. "I've nevah been heah before."

"And your reticence is understandable." he replied. "But I promise you, you will not come to harm."

I turned to my elf. "Whaddaya think?"

"I think...I think we don't have a choice." she whispahed, leanin' against me. Her right arm was cradled to her chest like it was broken.

"Hey. You all right?"

"Of course she's not." thah demon growled. "She's killed an angel. That is a crime few commit with impunity."

Kieran's eyelids stahted flutterin' an' I moved to support more of her weight. She didn't look so good.

"What thah fuck is wrong with her? She ain't gonna die or anythin'...right?"

"Unless you start trusting me, she might."

"What ah we waitin' for? Staht thah damn pahty."

"You are so eager to help your enemy?" thah demon asked, leadin' us inside.

I glared at the elf who had nursed me, fled with me, an' saved my sohry ass. "Thah elves may be my enemy, but she ain't. What's wrong with her?"

"Did her skin come into contact with the angel's blood?" our host rattled around some glass vials.

I eased Kieran onto thah edge of thah demon's couch. She looked at me in thanks, those big black eyes goin' straight to my soul.

"Yeah, she did. What of it?"

Thah demon, Darrintek, he called himself, made a noise of undahstandin'.

"What's wrong with touchin' angel blood?" I wondered.

Darrintek took Kieran's pulse. I didn't like thah look on his face. "Angelic blood is holy. If anything unholy touches it, they will die."

"Fuck." I breathed. "So why don't angel blood kill demons?"

Darrintek smiled. "Because our blood is holy as well. Do you forget, witch, that once we were angels?"

He made Kieran lie back an' he laid her right arm across her stomach. She winced when he touched it.

"Nah. I remembahed that bit. So how was she able to kill an angel?"

"I don't know." he answahed at last. "I confess I find it delightfully baffling."

"Why?" I seemed to be askin' that question a lot lately.

"Because there is only one other race to ever fight with angels, kill angels, and walk away unharmed."

"Yeah," I was a little suhprised, "which one? Thah vamps?"

"Oh no." thah demon began rubbin' some sort of salve on Kieran's arm. I hoped it helped.

"Which one then? Thah weres?"

"Wrong again." violet eyes smirked at me. "The humans."

Collision and Confusion – Aislyn

I didn't like it here. Wolf didn't either. She bit and kicked and clawed and howled and drove me damn near crazy. The air smelled like sulfur and felt electric. It was cold too, windy and drizzling.

"What's wrong, mutt?" Judah asked.

"Nothing." I didn't want him to think I was weak. "I've just never been to hell before."

"Not many have." he sounded all broody. "I myself find it rather peaceful."

"Not me." I breathed, rather startled that he had opened up.

It wasn't like him to share. He hadn't said a damn word when we'd found that dead angel. The sight of death was nothing to him, I knew, but seeing something that beautiful and powerful just gone…was *horrible*. I didn't care how long you'd been alive, that atrocity should affect you.

"Where are we going?" I asked, looking around.

Every street was a maze of craziness and confusing patterns.

"We're going until we're discovered." he informed me. "In hell, you don't find anything. It finds you."

*So that makes me prey…*I thought. Wolf bucked at that, clawing me apart from the inside, tearing at the seams of consciousness and skin.

I gasped at the sudden pain and stopped, trying to control myself. I would not become that beast. Not here, not in front of a damn leech.

"Are you all right, mutt?" he asked.

Those forest eyes raked me over and I knew he could smell the sweat on my skin.

"Fine." I ground out through teeth that were trying to become fangs.

"Your dual nature is not helping you, is it?" he actually sounded concerned, or at least interested.

"Wolf is not comfy in hell." I managed, dropping to my knees as my bone structure rippled.

"Am I going to be forced to carry you?" he asked.

Anger made me get to my feet. "No." I dusted my jeans off. "I'm good."

"Very well." he started walking again. "Don't slow me down, mutt."

Wolf growled deep in my throat. She didn't like hell and she didn't like him. "I'm not a mutt." I grumbled.

I jogged up to the leech and kept pace with him. The air shifted and cracked. Judah dashed to the side and I followed, watching the atmosphere split.

All of a sudden, a god-awful *beautiful* man stood there with us. He had hair whiter than white, and gorgeous, soulful violet eyes. Hands with delicate pianist's fingers adjusted a perfectly tailored suit. I swallowed. No wonder demons were masters of temptation. They looked *good.*

"Darrin!" Judah yelled at the demon. "It's about time you showed. What in hell is going on?"

The demon smiled, blinding me with teeth almost as white as his hair. "Judah, I've been expecting you. Don't be rude and insult your host. Who is your friend?"

"The angels sent me with a mutt." Judah snarled.

I bristled, fed up with the insult. "I'm not a mutt." I explained, but the demon didn't hear me. He was too busy laughing.

"This is beautiful." he grinned. "Vampire and werewolf partners, elves who kill angels, witches who won't kill elves. Vicious angels and clueless humans. It's brilliant!"

"Explain." Judah ordered.

"In time." he promised. "There is much to tell. Follow me. You are not safe here."

The atmosphere split open again and the demon extended his arm, inviting us to walk through. I sighed. Hell sucked.

Purgatory – Kieran

"What do you want with me?" my voice feels weak, tired.

"Just some information." says a soothing tone. "Tell us what we need to know, and you'll be allowed to rest."

No, I think. **Don't listen to him. He lies. Every time. Witches don't tell the truth. But I'm so...so tired. Haven't slept in...three—is it three—yeah. Three days.**

"What is your name?"

"Kieran."

"No clan name? All elves have clan names. This doesn't have to hurt, Kieran. We've been over this before. What is your full name?"

"Kieran."

Fire rips across my ribs. The witch holds a strip of my own skin in front of me. "Really, elf? Is this necessary?"

Cold air strikes the exposed bone of my ribs, stinging. The witch lifts a bottle of clear liquid in front of me. "Still no sound, **Kieran***?" he asks. "Did they tell you to be brave? Did they bring you up on tales of heroism in the face of pain?"*

I keep my lips closed. If I open them, I don't know what I will say, who will I endanger?

"They're lying to you, Kieran. It's not a crime to acknowledge pain. And there is no shame in ending it. Please, for your sake. We'll ask easier questions. What do you know of the Redblade blood witch?"

Wait...this is no nightmare. *Fear vibrates up and down my spine.* **It's some sort of...dream state reality. Oh goddess no! Why is this happening again?!**

"I don't know that name."

The clear liquid, vodka, splashes into the open wound. I gritted my teeth, turning the scream in my throat into a low growl. "You do know that name, Kieran. You don't have to lie. It won't help you."

I'm shaking now, shaking with pain and exhaustion and fear. I know what comes next. It's much much worse.

"I don't know that name." I re-iterate.

"Kieran, it's pointless. We know you know her. Now tell us, did you kill the seraphim. Or did she?"

"I don't know what you're talking about."

I clench my fists, feeling the cold tang of metal against my bone.

"Please, Kieran." the witch entreats, trying to sound sympathetic. "You don't have to endure this. Who killed the angel?"

"I don't know what you're talking about."

The witch sighs and gives the signal. I hammer crashes down on the chisel that rests on my ribs. I scream...

Scary Revelations — Mia

I'm in hell. I'm in hell with a hot demon an' an angel killin' elf who shouldn't be able to do what she did. Goddess, I hope she's okay.

I meandahed intah thah kitchen an' poured myself a cup of coffee. Hmmm...Stahbucks could learn a thing or two from coffee in hell. Howevah, knowin' it was a demon's brew would prob'ly turn away potential customahs.

How did I get heah? I spared a moment to wondah. *Stahted out in heaven an' it took me to hell. Gotta admit it ain't horrible heah...but I hope I don't gotta stay.*

An eah splittin' shriek had me runnin' from thah kitchen to thah livin' room. Thah elf was starin' up with eyes that didn't see, her skin was white as a fuckin' sheet an' her hands clenched so tightly that her nails had drawn blood.

"Holy shit." I breathed.

Kieran's skin felt cool to thah touch, but she was sweatin' like she had a fevah. "Kieran, honey, can ya heah me?"

Wheah thah fuck is she? What did killin' that angel do to her?

"I don't know what you're talking about." Kieran said, her eyes closin'.

"Who's talkin'?" I hated feelin' so weak, so useless.

I was a blood witch, dammit, with access to far more powah than most witches, an' I couldn't do jack shit.

"I don't," Kieran coughed, an' feah sliced through me as blood trickled from between her lips, "know any Redblade witches."

"Oh fuck." I undahstood, or at least I thought I did.

Somethin' was rippin' intah her head, wreakin' havoc an' tearin' her apaht. My guess would say it was angels.

Fuckin' angels, man.

Kieran's brow crunched an' a growl slipped out from between her clenched teeth. Whatevah was goin' on, it had to fuckin' *hurt*. Elven fighters were stoic; they didn't flinch, they didn't show pain, they didn't make noise. I knew that, so lookin' at her like this made my gut clench.

Tryin' not to hurt her, I sat down on thah couch an' eased her onto my lap. Her head leaned against my shouldah; I wrapped my arms around her as she stahted to shake.

"Wake up, Kieran." I begged. "Stop lettin' them hurt you. Hell, give me up if it gets you outta theah."

"I won't," Kieran whispahed, "tell you anything."

My heart broke when I saw teahs slip from between closed eyes. *Why thah fuck is she doin' this? Makes no fuckin' sense whatsoevah. How is makin' a damn mahtyr of ya'self gonna change anythin'?*

I thought of wheah I stood, how I caught myself starin' at her smile, found myself wantin' to heah her voice, looked at her just to see thah glow in those black velvet eyes. Hell, maybe she was changin' things.

...to thah drastic point wheah a witch stahts to fall for an elf...

60

"Holy mothah of thah cross-eyed gods." I breathed, lookin' at thah tortured woman in my arms. "I did *not* just think that."

But my own mind knew itself. *Yeah. Ya did.*

I am no lover of pain, but a believer in its necessity. Though, strangely, the knife I have driven into my back plagues me with guilt. Watching suffering, feeling only discomfort.

I read tales of betrayal, the exquisite anguish driven deep into the heart and soul, so painful that words fail to illuminate, so deep that if one were to dive into it their lungs would be crushed.

I have been betrayed, and watched the ones I love tortured and tormented. I feel as all feel, but can do nothing. I desire as all desire and I am left hollow.

What...what is wrong with me; what is broken inside? My Messiah, my beautiful, encompassing dream, where are you when my soul screams in the dark of night? Where are you at all?

Pages of Regret – Judah

"Please, have a seat." Darrintek spoke to the mutt.

She sat down, looking ill at ease. Were I her, perhaps I would feel the same. I was no longer young, and rarely discomfited by anything.

"You will be all right." I told her, trying to remember the depth of emotion required to reach mortals. "We can trust him."

"Right now I don't trust myself." she said.

Her voice quavered and she still looked pale. Her wolf must have been going mad.

"Then try to trust me." I attempted to sound reassuring. She nodded and closed her eyes.

"So innocent." Darrintek mused. "How did she wind up enmeshed in this wicked spider's web?"

"In the same manner as I." I replied, adjourning with the demon to another room. "The angels have something she values more than sanity."

"And they offered you your one true desire." Darrin frowned. "You didn't refuse."

"You advised me not to."

"And I applaud your decision, Judah. You have furthered this epic plot."

"Plots aside," I glanced around, examining the room, "why are we not at your home?"

"Ah!" he smiled. "When I saw you with the wolf, I thought it unwise to take you there. The young are so impetuous, you know."

"Darrintek, are you by any chance—"

"Harboring a blood witch and an elven angel killer?" he grinned, full of black intent. "Judah, I'm offended that you would think to look elsewhere."

"Why? Why when you know—"

"Because these are very old pieces in an ancient puzzle!" Darrin interrupted. "Judah, you have been beguiled into the oldest and most insidious of schemes. It was woven before the creation of the five races, when there were only angels and demons."

"I don't know what in hell you're talking about."

"Oh, it's not just in hell. It's on earth, and in heaven. The formula that has kept the world spinning is about to receive a blow to the equation that keeps history repeating."

My mind raced, an unusual and long forgotten sensation. Darrintek thrust sheaves of old paper in my hands.

"It's all there, Judah, every single documented attempt to turn the world on its end. All failures. But, they've introduced a new component this time. After centuries of attempts, they may finally have gotten it right."

"Gotten what right?" I asked, hating the sensation of confusion. "The formula to end the world?"

"Oh no, friend. The formula to change the world forever."

I dropped the papers on the floor, crossed my arms, and stared at the demon. "Explain."

Darrin smiled. "In due time."

He cut into the atmosphere and dashed away. I pursed my lips and walked back into the room. The mutt perked up and stared at me.

"What's going on?" she asked.

"Either we are the greatest thing since sliced bread," I answered, "or we are properly fucked."

Hell Within Hell – Kieran

"Please, Kieran, this doesn't have to continue." my torturer entreats. *"Is it so hard to answer simple questions?"*

"Examine," I look at my blood-stained body; force my voice to work, *"the evidence."*

"You are stubborn and foolish, elf." he cautions. *"But also remarkably brave."*

This... *my thoughts are sluggish...* **this is what I promised...that I would never again endure. Why...am I forced...to suffer?**

"Why are you and Mia Redblade conspiring against Heaven?"

"I have nothing to do with heaven."

The witch drives a glowing red spike through my foot. I scream again, knowing their methods have changed. I've almost lost too much blood...I'm no good if I'm unconscious. The heat will cauterize the wound.

And I will feel everything.

"You disgust me." my torturer says. *"Believing that you are helping her. Just tell us, Kieran. Tell us Mia Redblade killed the angel. The torture will stop; you'll forget that it happened. If only you had trusted us, none of this would have come to pass. End it, Kieran."*

End it...but I've fought so hard. I want to remember this, every excruciating moment. I want to remember.

"I know nothing." I say for the millionth time.

"Oh, fuck it." the witch growls.

He grabs a blade and drives it between my ribs, against my lung.

I gasp, feeling tears flood my eyes as the last blood I can stand to lose flows out. Surrendering, I let my eyes close.

I'm...sorry...

∞

Warmth...one radiating spot of warmth that tastes like cinnamon. Cinnamon and blood.

My eyes flared open, locking with lovely, worried blue ones…a gaze I recognize…from present and from past.

Mia flew back, scrabbling across the floor.

"I sweah to God I wasn't kissin' you!" she exclaimed. "You stopped breathin'! I sweah!" The fear in her eyes turned to concern. "Ah you okay? What was happenin' to you?"

"I," my throat was raw, "revisited some old memories."

The scratching in my throat made me cough. Pain wracked my body as fragile bones were jarred. Mia rubbed my back. When the spasm stopped, I lay still for a moment. If I didn't move, it didn't hurt.

I pulled my hand from my mouth, scared all over again when I found it covered in blood.

A Sort of Explanation – Aislyn

Silence made me uncomfortable. "Look," I stared at the leech, "the angels told me pretty much nothing. The demon has been just as helpful. As far as you know, what the fuck is going on?"

Judah returned my look, his powerful eyes going back into the centuries. "The Hinges of the World." he said. "Time itself. It's all been governed, from now until the end."

"Are you talking about God?" I asked.

The vampire smiled. "I suppose you could think of it as such. The angels call it Fate Path. And, as the overseers of the world and the races, they are bound to this Fate Path."

"What does that mean, though? Some sort of grand design?"

"In essence. Angels are required to follow Fate Path. Everything for them has been written in stone. Angels do not know what it is to feel as we feel. They desire nothing because their history is laid out for them. If they follow Fate Path, and they will, then our world is guaranteed to persist as it does."

"In turmoil and chaos and constant war?" I asked. "That's just...awesome."

"Ah, but you forget, mutt, that Fate Path has been broken before."

I realized what he meant after a second. "You mean when the demons were created. When they fell."

He nodded, actually looking pleased. "It put a dent in the flawless equation that spins our world. From what I know, the design was stabilized...by a great sacrifice made by Heaven. But such a sacrifice created loopholes, loopholes over which the angels and demons have been dueling for thousands of years."

"Why?" I inquired.

He had all this knowledge and I felt so stupid, which made me mad. But maybe he was thrown for a loop, because for once he wasn't condescending.

"Because if these loopholes are exploited, Fate Path will vanish, and possibly all of life with it. God dethroned. And both heavenly beings rather like living."

I smiled. The leech didn't make jokes that often. I didn't even know if he had a sense of humor.

"So why are we here?" I asked the question that had been preying on me since we entered hell.

Judah frowned. "That's what I don't know. Darrintek has the witch and the elf."

I jumped from my seat. "Then we have to find them!" I exclaimed. "And get out of here. Frankly, angels and demons can duke it out all they want, I just want my payment."

Judah nodded. "I want to hear Darrin's side of it first." he said.

Wolf growled deep in my gut. "Why?"

"Because in all the stories of Beginning I have heard, the five races did not come into being until after the Fall. And when they were created, Fate Path was set in place...so that angels might never again rebel."

A little confusion worm burrowed into my brain. "What...what does that mean?"

"What I hypothesize," he paced the room, "is that the angels have found a way to destabilize the equation...and they are selfish creatures."

"So you're saying..."

"That if the angels have their way with Fate Path, they alone will be left. The rest of us disappear."

I sat down again, winded. "Fuck."

Meeting with Enemies – Kieran

"Holy shit." Mia breathed. "Kieran, talk to me. What thah hell did they do to you?"

I stared, still transfixed by the bright red blood on my hands. "They," my voice sounded wet and thick, "asked me questions. About you. About the angel."

She brushed my hair out of my face. Her hand was so warm. "Did you tell them anythin'?"

"No." I started coughing again, feeling tears slip from my eyes as pain rattled through me. More blood splashed against my hands.

"What'd they do when ya didn't answah questions?" Mia asked, sitting down and positioning me where I could breathe easier; where she supported me.

I had never known a witch had the capability for kindness.

She is...so different from all of them...especially...no. I have forgiven him. And yet the witches paint her as dark, evil, a cancer amidst their ranks.

"Everything. Tore open my skin, chiseled my bones, broke fingers...hot pokers. Whatever you consider painful," I paused as my chest tightened, "they did."

"An' ya think thah angels pulled all this from your memory?"

"I know they did." I whispered, trying not to aggravate my cough. "Because they had a witch torturing me. I thought it was a simple nightmare until they started asking questions about you. And waking up to this," as if on cue, I started coughing, "...only proves that some of it was real."

"So you're what? Ripped up on thah inside?" her hands fluttered over my body, checking for open wounds.

"They...they stabbed me. The knife hit my lung. Not sure how bad the damage is."

"Fuck." she sounded pissed...and very sad. I wondered why.

Both of us started as the atmosphere split open and the demon entered the room. His violet eyes flew straight to Mia's. "How is she?" urgency colored his voice.

"I'm fine." I lied.

I wasn't fine. I wasn't even okay. But there was no way I was going to tell him that.

"Good." he breathed. "Something has happened to throw a wrench in Heaven's plans."

"What?" Mia asked.

"I have the catalysts with me. And I can explain everything. However, I do have to put you in contact with two certain individuals...individuals who are contracted to drag you back to Heaven, kicking and screaming if need be."

"They can try." I said. "I, for one, want some answers."

"Oh, lovely!" he exclaimed, stepping back through the tears in the world.

"So we're finally gonna find somethin' out." Mia stated, the look of aggravation she had worn leaving her face. "'Bout damn time. But ah you sure you're all right?"

"No." I stood up, hissing in pain and clutching my side. All the internal damage from torture was very, very real.

"Sit your ass back down before you teah ya'self in half."

I obeyed, still awed by her concern. I couldn't fathom for the life of me where it had come from.

"Just rest for now." Mia ordered. "Save ya strength. Then we can figuah out who's doin' what an' why, an' kick their ass from here to eternity."

"Okay." I agreed. The pain in my lungs intensified and I swallowed the urge to cough. "You win."

Mia laughed and let me lean against her once more. Then the room thundered and sulfur filled the air. Mia cursed and sputtered and I looked up to find the room filled with a demon, a vampire, and a werewolf. The acrid air caught in my throat and I started coughing again.

The pieces are falling together. Destinies on Fate Path intertwine. I have never touched that Holy Book, but in my soul I hear the song of triumph. Do you hear it, my Messiah?

In my house there are many rooms, and I have prepared a place for you. Your throne at my side is fashioned. Your name is written beside mine. After all this time, centuries of anguished waiting, you have come to me.

You have not rested in so long, and I hold peace that passes all understanding. As is everything of me, it is yours.

Now is the time. Now is the time for eternity to be set aright.

The Unveiling – Judah

The air reeked of sulfur. The wolf and I both hated it. Only Darrintek was unaffected, as usual. I looked at the couch, taking in with my senses the sight, smell, and sound of my quarry. Darrin had said this meeting must be peaceful, but I had lived long enough to see how quickly the status quo could change.

This witch was a true beauty, phosphorescent blue eyes and hair the color of rich earth. The tiny dent in her chin added a roguish look to an overall serene face. She smelled of cinnamon, unlike most witches, who were not strong enough to smell of the magic they used. I decided I liked her.

The elf was coughing. That didn't surprise me. Sulfur was not pleasant, especially to the elves. What did surprise me was the smell of blood. The mutt scented it too, and we exchanged wary glances. Perhaps they had not left the fight with the angel unaffected.

Other than that, the elf struck my eyes with a...peculiar loveliness. Raven hair and matching eyes that held untold sorrow and compassion. But that scar on her face—that scar held stories. I wanted to know them.

What a strange pair they made, sitting together on a demon's couch. Almost as strange, I glanced at the mutt, as she and I. *Well.*

"Judah, Aislyn, meet Mia and Kieran. Together, you four have successfully upfucked the world."

"But how?" the witch asked. "All I know is that thah angels wanted me for some experahment. It's why I cut an' ran."

"You escaped from Heaven?!" the mutt exclaimed. "That's...that's impossible."

"Yeah, but I'm magical." she snapped.

I cracked a smile a at the witch's horrid pun. If anything at all good happened here, it was the renewed sense of life I felt stirring in me, the return of emotion that I longed for.

"So tell us why we're here, Darrintek." the elf's voice was tired, blood-soaked. Whatever road had brought us here had not been easy for her.

"Fate Path is set." my friend began. "It is what governs the world. Whatever has been was written in it, whatever will be is known to the Scribe. All the world is set in motion, but it stands on a faulty foundation."

We listened, the wolf and I hoping that what we had been promised would be true.

"The first flaw in the foundation was created by the Fall. Renegade angels and curious humans are responsible for the disaster your world has become. However, even our rebellion was marked in Fate Path. The equation is so perfect as to allow functionality even after its destabilization, even though some sacrifice was required. And the Eyes of Eternity watch. These centuries spent in imperfection are punishment. But punishment is not eternal. Fate Path calls a Messiah, one who will set the equation aright, close all loopholes. It must be one who was born to see the mortal world to its end."

I glanced at the elf. Her kind were immortal. Was she this world's Messiah?

"It must also be one," Darrin grew grave, "who has forsaken this birthright. This is why I have brought you all together. Judah," he turned to me, violet eyes alight, "your one true desire, the one promised to you by Heaven, is the return of your human soul."

Something very akin to worry slithered through my veins.

"And the only way to receive this is to bring these two," he gestured to the witch and the elf, "before Heaven."

I wouldn't answer, but the mutt nodded for me.

"So take them." he offered, standing aside to where I had a clear view of the two renegades.

"What thah fuck!" the witch jumped up from the couch, blue eyes blazing. "Ya said we were all chill heah?"

Darrin laughed, freezing the room. "You think I care about you?" he asked the witch. "That I, who have scraped and scrounged and fought to survive the millennia, would care for a mortal's fate? Judah's desire and Heaven's promise will return to him his mortality."

Heavenly song surrounded us, and the roof of the building exploded upward. The room swarmed with glittering angels holding golden shackles. One dropped a leather pouch into Darrintek's hands.

"As agreed." the angel rumbled.

My demon, my friend, my betrayer, gazed at me with gleaming, hopeful eyes. As angels lifted me towards Heaven, his whisper floated past my ear.

"Judah...you are...the Messiah."

"This is so many levels of not good." I muttahed, pacin' thah floorh of my cell.

It wasn't a bad cell by any means, more like a hotel room, but a cage is a cage an' thah two of us knew it.

I walked ovah to Kieran. She didn't look good at all. Her skin was white as fuckin' snow, cold to thah touch, but she was still sweatin'. She hadn't stopped coughin' blood eithah. That's what worried me thah most.

"You hangin' in theah?" I asked, lookin' for somethin', anythin' in those black eyes that would tell me it was all right.

"I'm good." she answahed, holdin' my gaze.

Good doesn't mean all right, I thought.

"Do ya think what thah demon was sayin' is true?" I asked.

"It wouldn't surprise me." she whispahed. "But it seems definite that Judah is this Messiah figure. He fits the parameters. So I don't understand why you and I," she coughed an' I winced at thah sound of her rattlin' breath, "are here."

"'Cause thah fuckin' angels didn't like me gettin' away. An' you're screwed too, Kieran. Fuck it. Ya nevah shoulda helped me."

She wiped blood from her lips an' my heart ached.

"Yet I can't help but think I did the right thing."

I almost said it. I almost let those three devastatin' words come out of my mouth. But I didn't. I was afraid. It was **way** too soon.

Some stupid-ass blood witch who fucks ya life up an' gets ya tortured by angels says "I love you," then things get even worse.

So. I kept my mouth shut.

"I hope so." I replied, instead of what first came to mind. "Whaddaya think this Messiah thing is about?"

"If Darrintek is right," Kieran mused, "then all of the things that the angels think are wrong with the world are about to be remedied. It will be their return to Paradise."

"Sounds pleasant." I nodded. "But somethin' still stinks about this whole thing."

"Yes. It does."

I looked her ovah, thah exhaustion in her face, pain in her eyes. I didn't get it. Elves were immortal. She shoulda been well on her way to healin' herself. But she wasn't, and I didn't feel comftahble askin' why.

"Get some rest." I told her. "We won't know anythin' 'til they tell us."

She lay down with a pained sigh that made me hurt.

"Okay."

Fondest of Dreams – Aislyn

"Come this way, Aislyn." the angel floated in front of me.

I followed her through the blinding hallways. Wolf hated the smell. All sterile and sharp, like a hospital. I didn't like it either.

The angel led me to a tiny room and asked me to sit down. I did, feeling nauseated as wolf rattled around inside me, pacing, howling, clawing.

"Are you all right?" the angel asked.

"Yeah. I'm okay." I answered. "I just don't like small spaces."

"I understand, but it is only for a short while. Please, wait here."

She left and I sat in the room, waiting. There was nothing on the walls, not even the stale little pictures like they have in doctor's offices or hotel rooms. The air was cold and conditioned and...stale. Fake. I thought this little room felt worse than hell.

But I'm in Heaven, I thought. *Something is not right here.*

I stood and paced the four walls of the room, watching, hearing, feeling the bones in my hands crackle as they tried to change. I took a deep, calming breath.

"All that is nearly behind you." I heard a beautiful voice and turned to face it. Josephine, the Secretary of Angelic Affairs, smiled down on me. "Your fears, your pain, all the trauma your dual-nature has caused you to endure. You have done what was asked of you, and you will receive your reward."

"You'll get rid of the wolf?" I asked, not ready to allow myself to hope for the possibility.

"We will." she paused, and I sensed indecision.

"What aren't you telling me?" I asked.

"The procedure is more complex than I was led to believe." her over-bright eyes examined me. "In order to remove this burden from you, we will have to remove a part of your soul."

Wolf was clawing me apart inside. It **hurt**.

"You can do that?" I asked.

"It will take a little longer to prepare for the procedure, but yes, we will be able to do it. You won't be harmed, Aislyn."

"In that case," I gasped as Wolf gnawed at my organs, "what are we waiting for?"

She smiled that radiant smile and my soul felt warm. Even wolf calmed down a little.

"Feel free to return to your room. We will come for you when the preparations are finished. You should be proud of what you've done, Aislyn."

About that, I wasn't sure. "What's going to happen to the witch and the elf?"

Josephine looked…sad for some reason. "I am not yet certain."

Wages of Salvation – Judah

"My Messiah," the tone in the angel's voice bordered on worshipful. "We have waited for this moment since the beginning. We have waited for you."

Dark shadows swirled inside my mind, breaking like oil-soaked waves on a flaming shore. This one action, simple as it was, would set the world aright? Surely not.

I had never, in the centuries I had walked the earth, seen something changed with ease. Returning my soul would not rectify Fate Path.

But the schemes of angels meant nothing to me. I wanted my soul. It had been taken from me; had turned me into a monster. And, at last, after centuries, I would be restored.

"As I have waited for this." I replied. "Where is the Secretary?"

"The Secretary of Angelic Affairs will be with you in a moment. Your return and the presence of those you've brought with you have caused quite a stir."

I smiled, then remembered the ferocity of the witch's eyes, the pain in the elf's. "What will happen to the two I brought with me?"

"The witch will be reprimanded for rebelling against angelic authority and killing those sent to retrieve her. As for the elf...we are not certain. We believe she killed one of our own...angels are not executioners by nature but such a crime—"

"Cannot go unpunished." I finished.

The two were doomed to Heaven's justice. And their punishment had purchased my soul. Perhaps that sacrifice was enough to set Fate Path aright. Only blood fed the world.

"You are wise, vampire." the angel smiled. "When Josephine arrives, you will receive what you have longed for, my Messiah."

The title still felt wrong to my ears. My heart, such as it was, rejected it. I had done much wrong. I had killed, maimed, tortured, all in the name of pleasure. Somewhere, deep within, I knew I was not the one to redeem the world.

I leaned back in my chair, grateful that this time it was not playing music. I could not, within myself, justify the impatience I felt. After centuries, it seemed strange that a few minutes dragged for a seeming eternity.

The door opened and a flash of red hair caught my eye. I sat up, hoping. But then I smelled dog.

"What do you want, mutt?" I asked.

"I was waiting for them to be ready." Aislyn grinned, looking so young. "And I smelled you. So I thought I'd say 'hi'. You're about to become human, after all. That means I have to protect you...I mean...until I'm human again too."

I smiled at the notion of this slip of a girl protecting me. "I do not mind if you wish to stay."

She grinned and sat down in another chair. "I wonder what paradise will be like." she thought out loud. "All the flaws in the world made perfect again. I don't believe it will get rid of us all, Judah."

"I hope you're right."

The door swung open again. Josephine entered, gleaming. Her eyes glittered when they rested on me, but I didn't care about the hope in them. What I cared about was the shivering silver glow in her hands that resonated with my thoughts and called to me.

"Messiah." she said, bowing.

"Madame Secretary." I greeted her. "Please rise."

She did, and smiled. "Rest in your mind, Judah." she ordered. "And know that you shall become whole again. And with you, the world."

The hand that held glowing silver planted itself against my chest and drove itself inside. I screamed as light irradiated me, bringing with it renewed sense of emotion and feeling. But...something was wrong...missing. A part of me...the part of my soul that killed this infection, that made me human...wasn't there.

My eyes pierced a hole through Josephine.

"It didn't work." I gasped, clutching my chest as a new pain overtook me.

Hunger.

My fangs flashed down. I was still a vampire, with half a human soul.

Josephine drew back as I reached for her. I recoiled...remembering. If I fed from her, I would die.

The room still smells of dog.

"Judah," Aislyn's tiny voice, "are you all right?"

I reached for her faster than thought, brought her neck to my lips, and sank my teeth into her veins.

Walking with Death – Kieran

"Kieran, Kieran, honey, wake up."

I open my eyes, see raven ones looking into them.

"Mom?" I ask. "How am I here?"

Her hand flies to my forehead. "Are you feeling well?"

I remove her hand and squeeze it. "I'm all right. It must have been a bad dream. Very vivid though."

"Well, it's over now." she smiles and ruffles my hair. "Time to get up. We have a wedding to get ready for."

I get out of bed, surprised that I feel strong and not at all tired. I have not felt this good since before the war...and its aftermath. I turn on the sink and wash my face, looking in the mirror to examine my scar. I gasp...

It isn't there.

I put my hand to my face and feel for the change in texture. Nothing...just smooth skin. "Mother!" I call.

She bustles into the room. "What is it, honey?"

"Mom, where is my scar?"

She looks bewildered, almost angry. "What are you talking about?"

I look into the mirror; back at my mother. "I have a scar," I trace the line where it should be, "right here. From the witches who captured me."

"Witches?" mom asks. "Sweetheart, we haven't fought the witches in years. I don't know what you're talking about."

"Mom, you have to believe me." I beg, hating the strange feeling of the walls closing in on me. "I don't know what's happened, but this isn't right."

"Kieran, slow down. Breathe. We'll figure this out."

Frustration builds to a blowout point. "No!" I shout, slamming the side of my fist into a mirror.

Glass cracks and my skin with it. My mother grabs my bleeding hand and pulls the glass out of my skin.

I stare down at the cuts, watching the wounds as they immediately stop bleeding and slowly begin to close over. I start crying, knowing for certain what I had feared.

"This isn't real." I whisper, watching as the wounds finish closing. "Mom, I'm sorry. I wish I could stay. But this isn't real."

"Kieran," my mother looks up, tears in her eyes, "stay with me. This is real if you let it be. Just stop fighting, sweetheart. Stop fighting."

"I can't, mom." I close my eyes and will away the beauty of the dream. "Please, forgive me."

∞

"Kieran, open ya eyes or I sweah I will pull your eyelids up and glue 'em theah!"

"Mia." I whispered, relieved that I was free from the dream.

"Wheah thah hell were you?" she asked, refusing to look me in the eye.

"I was in heaven." I felt tears on my cheeks again.

"Whaddaya mean?"

"I was home, with my family. I had no scars, no pain, no injuries. I knew it wasn't real, but I wanted it to be."

"Why?" I could hear the sardonic smile in her voice. "Ya don't like it heah?"

"It's not that." I grinned, coughing a little. "In the dream...I was still immortal."

Like a Nightmare, Only Real – Aislyn

Oh god it hurt. Like drinking glass or diving in boiling water or going through a wood chipper.

"Ju...dah." the syllables caught in my weak voice as my vision blurred out to red.

"In the name of Heaven, get off of her!" Josephine commanded, grabbing Judah's shoulder and slamming him backwards.

I screamed as his fangs tore out of my skin and I fell from shock. Judah held the wall, staring around in confusion as I lay on the floor, gasping for air, holding my neck as blood streamed through my fingers.

"What's going on?" he asked. "I smell blood. Aislyn..."

"Don't touch her!" Josephine warned. She knelt beside me. "Aislyn, can you keep pressure on the wound?"

"I..." Wolf thrashed inside, howling in pain, "think...so."

He said my name, I thought. *The first time he hasn't called me mutt. Oh this is bad...bad bad bad bad bad bad bad.*

"Judah, get out." Josephine commanded in angelsong. "Find your peace somewhere. There is still much to do."

Judah ran out of the room, looking scared. Josephine removed my hand from the bloody mess of my neck.

"Aislyn, this is a bad wound. We need to get you into surgery. Do you understand what I'm saying?"

Her face started zooming in and out. Wolf shrieked inside, but even she wasn't strong enough to stop this.

"I get it." my voice sounded far away.

"If you like," she lifted me in arms too strong, "we will fulfill our part of the bargain as well."

"Yes." I whispered, watching white replace everything else I saw.

The angels would save my life…in exchange for my soul.

There is chaos in Heaven, my darling. This is not how I wished to greet you, with blood on my hands and sorrow in my voice. I wanted to be beautiful for you.

You, whom I have loved from the Beginning.

Why do you run, I ask myself. Why can I offer you nothing you desire when I hold all the world? What have I done wrong, my savior, my truth?

Will you answer me at last? I know you are near. I sense you, not in the broken vessel that wears your title, but in the tormented body awaiting...me. When our eyes meet, will you know? Will you know me as the one who has loved you from the first?

Holy Shit! Really? – Mia

Thah world spun all crazy for a minute an' I stared at Kieran. "Care to rewind that a little?"

Kieran smiled, but it wasn't a happy one. "In my dream, I was immortal again."

"Again?" I asked. Elves were born with immortality. It wasn't somethin' that just...went away. "Whattah ya talkin' about?"

Thah quiet scared me. Kieran had nevah hesitated to answah a question. It scared me even more when I saw that she was cryin'.

"Ya don't have to say if ya don't wanna." I covahed, hopin' I hadn't majorly fucked up.

"No." she whispahed; coughed a little. "I need to tell someone." She traced thah scar on her cheek an' I saw the horror of thah memory in her eyes. "I never told my family. They aren't ready. But...you know what this scar is...where it's from."

Sadness engulfed me. "It's an exit wound." I answahed. "A life-drain spell. Shoulda killed ya."

Kieran nodded. "Instead, it took my immortality." she said. "It tore me away from my eternal connection to the earth; it raped everything elven in me. I'm practically..."

"Human." I breathed, undahstandin' at last. "That's how ya killed thah angel."

"I didn't escape unscathed." she said, then coughed long an' harsh as if to remind me.

I rubbed her back, not likin' thah way her body shook.

"No, ya didn't. But that's how you were able to do it."

"I know." she looked so damn sad! "I figured it out after a little while." Teahs stahted fallin' from those gorgeous black eyes. "Mia, my mother will bury me. I will only live a human lifespan. My connection is gone. My heritage is destroyed. My brothers and sisters will live forever and have families and their families will have families and I will be dead!"

My heart went out to her, longin' to take all her pain an' carry it myself. My people had done this to her. Thah ones I called family had burned her life away. An' theah was nothin' I could fuckin' do about it.

"Thah mortal coil ain't so bad." I whispahed, not darin' to share that I wanted to spend my mortality near her.

"I know." she replied, lookin' off intah the distance of the life she could...should have had. "But sometimes it's too much. I miss the voices of my people all around. They used to surround me like a symphony. Now I walk in a world without music."

I looked at her, seein' how she was music. Her words were thah lyrics an' her voice was thah symphony. How could my people destroy this? An' how could she fohgive us an' not hold a grudge?

"Why in hell did you become a warrior?" I found myself askin'.

"Because I had too." she smiled. "And I wanted to make a difference. Besides...sometimes you have to be inside the beast to kill it."

I could have kissed her theah an' then, but that would have been awkwahd.

But most witches nevah take thah time to see innah beauty. We're so focused on spellcraft and shit outside thah heart an' soul. But here I sit, seein' somethin' amazin' right in front of me. An' I nevah wanna look at anythin' else evah again.

Re-Damned – Judah

What in heaven and hell is happening to me? I stared at my—my reflection. I had not seen my reflection in centuries. I had not expected to be startled when I saw my face again. But I was.

Now you must come face to face with who you are, my thoughts whispered.

"I don't want to." I said, wiping blood from my chin. "I do not know what I am anymore."

"***Decide.***" Darrintek's harsh voice rang inside my thoughts. "***Choose who you are. Murderer or Messiah?***"

"Am I not both?" I asked, not questioning my friend's intrusion into my mind. He had done so before. "Even now, this newly-ensouled travesty is fighting for a title and a name. I do not know if I have done the right thing. I sold someone to regain something that no longer exists."

"***Judah, you are saving our world.***" Darrin pressed. "***This ensoulment will equalize the Fate Path equation. You are the immortal who became mortal. You are the Messiah!***"

"You don't understand!" I roared, shattering the mirror with my fist. "Something was *missing*, Darrin! I'm not human. I can feel. I can see my reflection but my heart does not beat and I still thirst for blood. I...I almost killed the mutt."

"***What in hell is going on up there?***" my demon wondered.

"You tell me." I said, dry. "You're the one who sold me out to them."

"***And didn't you get what you wanted?***" he asked. "***Did you not regain your soul?***"

"But nothing is as you've said." I replied, trying to calm myself with musings and logic. It had carried me through decades of pointless existence. "The angels have mentioned nothing of what you spoke. They have called me the Messiah, but nothing more."

I could hear him frown. "*This makes less and less sense. The Secretary and I had an agreement. I give her the messiah, she equalizes the equation by giving you your soul.*"

"Which they did." I said. "But it only restored my humanity. It did not return my mortality!"

"*Oh, dear.*" Darrin's cultured voice turned worried. "*Now you have me upset. This is not good.*"

I stared at my fractured reflection in the splintered mirror. "You're right." I agreed. "You're very, very right."

Inner Nature – Aislyn

"Aislyn, my dear, are you awake?" I could make out the words, but they were coming from very far away.

"Yeah." that one word took everything out of me.

Wolf whispered…wait…she wasn't supposed to be here anymore. Panic triggered adrenaline and I struggled to sit up.

"What's…going…on?" I panted.

"Aislyn," the faraway voice cautioned, "you just came out of surgery. You're very weak. Please, lie back down."

That voice—that was angelsong, the impossible-to-resist voice of angelic command. I wanted to listen, but Wolf was having none of it. She bit and clawed and fought…and me, the Aislyn part of me, was too weak to fight her.

I gritted my teeth and ripped the IV out of my vein. The angel-medic protested as I staggered past her, but I couldn't hear her words as my bones melted and skin buckled.

My jaw ached as it extended, as human teeth became weapons of death. The world took new shape to different color eyes and with one blink…I was no more.

∞

I AM FREE. I AM GLORIOUSLY ALIVE AND UNLEASHED. THE VESSEL WHO BORE ME IS WEAK. THE LEECH HAS TAKEN HER BLOOD AND THE ANGELS HER SOUL. SHE WISHES TO BE RID OF ME, BUT I AM USEFUL YET.

I AM HER AVENGER. I AM HER PROTECTOR. I LOVE HER, BUT SHE HATES ME, MY NATURE, THE ESSENCE OF HER CURSED PEOPLE; THE ONE WHO TOOK VENGEANCE AGAINST HER PARENT'S

MURDERERS. BUT I WILL NOT ABANDON HER. SHE IS MINE.

I CAN SENSE AS SHE DOES NOT. THERE ARE DARK THINGS AFOOT, FOREIGN SMELLS, DANGEROUS SPIRITS, PHANTOM PAINS. ALL IS NOT WELL IN HEAVEN. SHE KNOWS THIS NOW, NOW THAT SHE IS TOO WEAK TO RUN, MUCH LESS TO FIGHT. THAT IS MY PURPOSE. TO FIGHT FOR THOSE WHO CANNOT.

"The…witch…" SHE WHISPERS INSIDE MY MIND.

I WILL NOT DENY HER VOICE, THOUGH SHE BEATS MINE INTO SUBMISSION. WITCHES KNOW SOMETHING OF SOULS AND SPIRITS. THEY ARE DARK CREATURES, BORN OF FIRE AND POWER…THEY SEE NONE BUT THEMSELVES. BUT IN HEAVEN, THE ANGELS ARE NOT OUR ALLIES.

WE MUST TRY MEASURES MORE EXTREME. THE SCENT OF CINNAMON TICKLES MY NOSE AND I FOLLOW IT, WORRIED BY THE UNDERLYING SMELL OF ELVEN BLOOD. WHOEVER THIS WITCH IS, I PRAY THAT SHE IS DIFFERENT FROM THE OTHERS…OR AGAIN MY FANGS WILL TASTE BLOOD IN THE DEFENSE OF MY BELOVED.

A Witch's Mercy – Kieran

"I wonder what's going on out there." I said, feeling the harshness of my voice.

The cough had eased a little, but I didn't know if it was a good or bad thing at this point. I decided to be grateful in the meantime and worry about it later.

"Chaos an' destruction." Mia said. "I don't like it. I'd really like to get you outta heah."

The worry in her eyes struck me. In such a short time, these insane circumstances had brought me close to someone I never would have known otherwise. Funny, how this had started out with *me* saving *her* life.

"Mia," I whispered, "thank you."

She turned to me, shock in her eyes this time. "For what?"

"For taking care of me." I answered, enjoying the light that crept into her smile. "And staying with me, even if I am an elf."

"It was my pleashah." she grinned, her tone as genuine as I had ever heard it. "I still owe ya for savin' my ass."

I laughed. "I think you've more than repaid that debt."

She looked a little awkward. "I think I owe ya a lot more." she said. "'Cause of what they...my people...did to you."

"I've moved beyond that." I said, amazed that I found it true.

I opened my mouth to say something else, but I started coughing, worse than before. It felt like someone had taken my lungs and squeezed all the air from them. Unable to breathe, I went to my knees.

Mia moved and knelt with me. Her hands steadied my shoulders. "Kieran. Breathe. Please breathe." It sounded like more of a wish than a command.

I opened my eyes and tried to smooth out the coughing. The spasm eased and I licked blood from my lips.

"You okay?" Mia asked, still massaging my back.

"I'm fine." I lied. *It's getting worse. And it won't get better any time soon. I won't heal from this.*

"Fuckin' angels." Mia cursed. "Who thah hell do they think they are, yankin' us from one place to thah next with no explanation?"

"I don't know."

She smiled. "Hope this doesn't piss ya off, but at least this time it's bettah...on me. I'm not alone anymore."

The underlying sorrow in her voice called to me but I did nothing. What could I do? She was a shunned witch already. It would be hoping too far to think she could harbor affection for a battle-scarred, mortal elf. I couldn't hope to give her the life her light deserved.

A rattle against the door took my mind from vain prayers and the strange gleam in Mia's eyes. The witch moved to the door. The rattle continued, followed by clawing sounds. Whatever it was, it was not an angel.

"Open the door." I said.

"It's not locked?"

"This is heaven and you're magicked out." I explained. "There's no way out of here unless they let you. They wouldn't lock their doors. It's a power play."

"That's fuckin' ridiculous." Mia said, turning the knob.

The door opened. A wolf staggered in; fell to the floor in front of Mia, whimpering.

"What thah fuck?" Mia's favorite phrase.

I laughed and regained my feet, kneeling once more beside the wolf. "It's her." I realized.

"Who?"

"The werewolf." I answered.

"Ya mean thah one that sold us out?"

I nodded. "She's been hurt."

"For bein' in heaven, my life sucks!" Mia exclaimed. "You're hurt, she's hurt, an' I think I'm goin' fuckin' crazy."

We watched as the wolf twitched and jittered, then transformed into a slender, red-headed girl once more. Her tear-filled eyes caught Mia's. "Please," she reached out with a trembling hand, "help me."

I glanced at Mia. Witches didn't hate werewolves as much as they did elves, but the two-natured were not high on the list.

"Whaddaya need?" Mia asked, and I smiled.

This is how the world can change.

"What happened?" Kieran helped thah wolf ovah to one of thah beds.

"I was...with Judah." she panted. She was all kinds of fucked up. "When they restored his soul."

Thah wolf stopped to breathe an' Kieran moved thah girl's hair away from her neck. Little railroad lines of stitches criss-crossed all ovah it.

"It didn't work." Kieran guessed. "He's still a monster."

Thah wolf shook her head; looked like she regretted it. "He's still a vampire. Not a monster."

I didn't undahstand why Kieran's face stahted glowin', but it did. Those velvet black eyes lit up an' sang. I could almost heah thah music an' it pissed me off. Thah world was crumblin' around my eahs an' I was swoonin' like a lovesick puppy dog.

Fuck!

"What happened, do you know?" Kieran asked. She sounded like she was soothin' a wounded animal.

Hell, in a way, she is.

"There...there was something missing." wolf girl took a deep breath. "His soul...missing...something important."

"Thah paht that made him human." I guessed. Kieran looked at me, puzzled. "I was up heah before." I explained. "I told ya they were fuckin' around with my soul. They even sliced a piece off it, nothin' majah...just weird as shit. But with thah vamp missin' a chunk of his..."

"Oh, my goddess." thah wolf breathed. "I think...I think they took part of mine. That's why I came to you." her frantic eyes grabbed mine. "Because you could tell me what they did."

I swallowed. "Why do ya think they soul-siphoned you?"

She hung her head. "I made a deal with the angels." she explained. "Like the vampire did. The Secretary of Angelic Affairs told me that if I helped them find you, they would take away the wolf. Before Judah...did what he did...I was told they would need a piece of my soul to remove her."

"But you still have the wolf." Kieran said. "So you want to know..."

"If they did nothing to my soul, or if they took a piece and left the wolf."

"This is so fucked up." I grumbled. "But I'll see what I can do. Close ya eyes an' hang tight." She obeyed an' I took her hand. "I gotta ask ya to relax. I know it's hahd, but let everythin' fall away. All you heah is my voice. Don't think about ya'self or about thah wolf. I'm not gonna let anything' hurt you."

"All right." she whispahed, an' actually let go.

That impressed me. It was tough to give ovah control of thought processes an' will. Then again, she had thah wolf. That made it easiah to detach one's conscious.

"Dammit!" I yelled when I finished. Thah wolf looked at me with puppy eyes.

"What'd they do to me?" she asked.

99

I ran my hand through my hair, tryin' to think of how to break thah news.

"Mia," Kieran's voice, coolin' thah fevah brewin' in my brain, "focus. We all have a great deal at stake in this."

"Ya ah missin' a chunk of ya soul." I admitted. "But they only suppressed thah wolf. They didn't cut her out. Frankly, sweetie, they can't. Thah wolf is a curse, an' curses ah fuckin' stamped in ya blood. Theah's no way to get rid of it."

Thah wolf looked at me like I'd pulled a strawberry out of a banana peel. "Then...they lied. The angels lied to me?"

I sighed. This was so many layahs of fuckin' twistedness that I was spinnin'. "They told ya they could get rid of it?"

She nodded, swallowed. "It's the only reason I agreed to find you and her." she gestured to Kieran.

"Aislyn, calm down." my elf cautioned. "You're frightened. We all are. You've lost a lot of blood; you're very pale, and you've been through surgery. You can't afford to over-exert yourself."

I pinched my lips. This was freakish. Angels stealin' soul slices like people were pizza. What thah fuck did they want with them? An' why had their "messiah" taken a bite outta wolf girl?

"Mia?" Kieran asked.

I looked at her, her eyes, thah scar, her blood-flecked lips. "Yeah?"

"She said they took a piece of Judah's soul. You said they took a piece of yours. Now Aislyn's. Do you know what they want?"

"If it's what I'm thinkin'," I said, "then we're fucked sixty ways from Sunday."

Blood stains the golden streets. There is fear in the eyes of those who were not born to that emotion. There is fear in my eyes. I am afraid. For you. Of you.

I have yet to see the fullness of Beauty, the essence of you. I feel your heart beats in tandem with mine. I want to love you.

I want to be free to love you.

But there is blood in Heaven. There are cries, and the equation is still set. The world is changing, yet I can find no catalyst. So I begin to ponder forgiveness. What is its nature, it causality? How is it earned? And will I ever need ask for it?

Demonic Conferences – Judah

I slammed through the office door with such strength that it tore from its hinges. The short angel who had let me into heaven the first time rose from his seat, flustered and red-faced.

"I need to speak with the Secretary." I informed him.

"You can't be here." he sputtered. "It's against regulations. I'll have to ask you to leave so I can file an incident report."

"Listen. To. Me." I demanded, grabbing the angel by his collar and lifting him off his feet. "I *need* to see the Secretary. We have to talk about this Messiah business. On the level."

"P...P...Project Messiah?" the tiny angel stammered. "The Secretary informed you of that?"

Project Messiah? I thought. *That does not sound like a prophecy. It sounds like a scheme.*

"Yes. I have been informed." I lied. "So you had better open that office door and let me speak with her. I am not afraid of angelic retribution."

"All right." he agreed, and I set him on the floor.

He shuffled to the office door and eased it open. "Pardon me, ummm, Madame Secretary, but you have an, ummm," he glanced back at me and I flashed my fangs, "an unhappy vampire in your lobby. He's demanding to speak with you."

A few moments of silence and the short angel re-emerged. "You may enter." he told me, trying to look down his nose at someone who stood a head and a half taller. "But I warn you, show some respect. She did restore your damned soul."

"Not enough of it." I quipped. I entered the office and looked back at the angel. "You might want to hold off on that incident report." I informed him. "I'm bringing a friend."

He jumped up and ran for the door. I took great pleasure in slamming it in his face.

"Judah," Josephine's pleasant tones, "I just got off the phone with the requisition department, concerning your soul. It turns out there was a slight problem with complete acquisition..."

"Do not give me the departmental tag line." I warned her. "I know the paper trail, when researched, will be flawless. Darrintek, come in please."

The air crackled, popped, and the demon appeared in the room. Shock spread over Josephine's face and she stood up behind her desk. "What is the meaning of this?" she demanded, looking from me to the demon and back again.

"Josephine! Darling!" Darrin exclaimed. "Don't be so angry. Check with your permissions department. You'll find I have authorized access through the Gate. You're not the only ruler of requisitions, you know."

Josephine went red in the face, but she sat down and leered. "Well, I have been thoroughly betrayed and invaded. What in God's name to you want?"

I took a seat in front of the desk and laced my fingers together. "I want you to tell me everything." I said. "About Project Messiah."

The Question of Why – Aislyn

"What do we know thus far?" the elf asked, sitting down as though she had no strength. She reeked of blood.

Mia, the witch, bit her lip. "We know thah angels ah playin' around with souls. We also know about some crazy ass recreation slash prophecy slash conspiracy about some sort of Messiah. But what thah fuck is a messiah gonna do? We know they're lookin' for one, maybe even found one, but we don't know why."

I huddled into myself like a cold puppy. I was afraid. I was in over my head, and I was freaking out. I didn't understand how the other two could be so calm.

"Have you anything to add, Aislyn?" Kieran, that was the elf's name, had a kind voice.

She was nice…and she was dying. Wolf could smell it and didn't like it. The elf, somehow, smelled like pack. Like good things.

"The angels aren't keeping their promises." I answered. "They didn't to Judah, and, according to Mia, they didn't to me."

"Lyin', cheatin', fuckin' bastahds." Mia kicked the wall. "There's a piece of my soul floatin' around out theah; I can feel it."

"Four people from four races." Kieran started coughing so hard and harsh it made me wince. The witch looked like she was in pain too. "The angels are collecting. Witch," she looked at Mia. "Wolf." she pointed at me. "Vampire." my thoughts went to Judah. "And elf." She paused to breathe. It took obvious effort.

"But they haven't soul-sucked you." Mia said, sitting down beside Kieran. It shocked me when the witch placed her arm around the elf in support.

"Yet." Kieran leaned her head on Mia's shoulder. "But they have an endgame that far outstrips the sum of its parts."

"So what are we involved in?" I asked. "Some sort of angelic conspiracy?"

"If only we knew what. And why." Kieran whispered.

"Wolf girl, ya ahn't lookin' so hot." Mia scanned me with her firecracker blue eyes. "An' ya ahn't one of us fugitives. Go an' get ya'self taken care of. Thah angels ahn't gonna do any more damage to ya than they already have. They may have lied to you, but they won't kill ya. They can't."

I stood up and walked to the door. In the past few days, I had seen the strangest things. Angels lying, demons telling the truth, vampires who weren't monsters, and a witch and an elf who weren't at each other's throats. The world was changing. It was frightening, but not unwelcome.

I glanced back at the elf. Wolf could sense there was more to her than met the eye. Her kind were immortal…but she was dying. And she was the only one who hadn't had their soul jacked around with.

"Mia."

The witch's eyes met my own. "Yeah?"

"Take care of her. I'm going to try to find Judah and see what he knows."

"You got it, wolf girl."

"Aislyn," Kieran's tired voice, "be careful. Right now, there is no one we can trust. In heaven or hell."

"Except each other." I tried to smile.

"Each other." Kieran's lips quirked upward.

Thah wolf left an' I sighed. "This is a fuckin' mess, Kieran."

"I know." she answahed, an' I felt more of her weight shift to me.

"You wanna lie down?" I asked, tryin' to ignore that my heart was beatin' fastah. With fear.

She wasn't gettin' any bettah. Her face had gone that sickish white color an' theah were bruises undahneath her eyes. Every breath she took seemed to take way too much effort.

"No." she shook her head. "If I go to sleep, I might not wake up."

That she said it so mattah of fact drove a sledgehammah in my gut. "How can ya do this?" I asked. "How can ya just sit heah, knowin' that thah damn angels wanna slice of ya soul, coughin' up blood, fightin' to breathe, an' talkin' 'bout not wakin' up!?"

"It's just death." she smiled, crackin' thah dried blood at thah cornah of her lip. "It's somewhere I've been before."

Thah wetness in my eyes scared me stupid. I wasn't supposed to cry. Why thah hell was I cryin'?

"You were gonna live forevah." I said. "An' you're more familiah with death than I am."

"And you," she coughed, "were the heir to a seat on the Red Coven council. Why did you jeopardize that?"

"How'd ya know?" I asked, shocked.

"It took me a while to p...piece it together." she told me. "My...my torturer talked to me...tormented me with stories of his family, knowing that the separation from mine was a fiercer torture than his knives and brands.

He knew how close I was to my sister, Reya. He would brag for hours on end about his twin sister, a witch of such talent and beauty that stood to inherit one of the most powerful seats on the coven council. His name was Micah. Micah Redblade."

Holy shit! My...my brothah was the one? He did this to her? He stole her from her family, tore up her body, an' ripped away her immortality? Fuckmothering son of a bitch!

"I'm sohry, Kieran." I whispahed, meanin' every word. She'd been so kind to me, all thah while knowin' who I was. "My brothah was good at his job...damn good. I know it takes a twisted sonnavabitch to be good at 'interrogation.'

But I loved him. Broke thah law for him. He got hurt when we were kids." I felt my eyes dry. I was done cryin' ovah this. "I was thah one who found him. Theah was no way to get help. So I did thah only thing I knew to do. I used my blood; I saved his life with blood magic. We kept it secret for yeahs.

But my cousin, fuckin' bastahd who'd been born to the wrong paht of thah family, wanted my seat. So he stabbed me in thah back by givin' my brothah a taste of his own medicine.

Witches can dish out pain...we suck at takin' it. Micah spilled his guts, an' that signed my death warrant."

"Your life has not been easy, Mia." Kieran said. Her breath felt warm against my skin. "I wish your road had been less troubled."

Thah damn watahworks in my eyes stahted again. "If I hadn't saved my brothah, you'd still be immortal. In a way..."

"I still would have been captured." she coughed an' caught thah blood spray against her hand. "And tortured. I blame no race, no person...no person that helped them. What happened to me can be laid at thah feet of a flawed world."

Goddess. She was so fuckin' beautiful, mind, body, an' soul. She shoulda had thah life she was born to— peaceful, quiet, forevah. An' yet heah she was with me, thah sistah of her torturer, waitin' in heaven on thah whim of angels and their fucked up schemes.

"We'll make it bettah." I promised, holdin' her closah to me.

Thah door burst open an' thah bitch I recognized as the one who'd done experahments on me stepped into thah room.

"Kieran Shandera, come with me, now."

"Mia," Kieran whispahed, "please help me stand."

My heart broke again. I rose an' helped Kieran to her feet. Two angels came an' snatched her away from me.

"Wheah ah you takin' her?" I asked.

Thah scahlet haired bitch glared at me. "That is not your concern, little witch." she glided out of the room with her goons in tow.

"Kieran!" I yelled, afraid that I might nevah look into those night sky eyes evah again. Thah angels stopped an' Kieran turned around, starin' straight into my soul."

"Yes."

"I...I love you."

Theah. I said it. Thah words were out theah, my heart on a tiny, tiny string. Whatevah happened next would strengthen or snap it.

"You are," she breathed, heavy, tired, full of sorrow, "such a light." Then she smiled, an' time went still. "Light in a world too long dark."

"Come, elf." an angel snapped.

I was freakin' out, but nothin' was gonna wipe thah huge smile off my face. I may not have realized thah exact meanin' of her words...but I undahstood thah way she said them, an' that gave me hope.

Come back to me, Kieran. Just come back to me. I sweah I'll nevah leave you.

"This is beyond demented!" Darrin fumed, pacing around the room. "Beyond conniving, beyond scheming, beyond sanity and lucidity! This is utter and complete..."

"Madness." I finished. "What sort of web have you tangled me in?"

He threw up his hands. "I don't know!" he exploded. "I thought I knew, and I was betrayed! What kind of Heaven is this, where angels lie and scheme and *steal!?*"

"I told you I was no Messiah!" I thundered. "I would have sworn it upon the blood of any god! I am a *monster*, Judah, not some legendary figure who would give up their mortality for unselfish reasons! And *you* betrayed me, Darrin! You sold me and made me sell another!"

"But listen to the passion in your voice." the demon persuaded. "Feel the bite, relish the familiar tang of emotion. You might not have gained all that you desired, but you do possess most of what you lacked."

"It's all wrong, though." a small voice intruded through the doorway.

Darrin and I both turned towards the words, shocked to see the mutt standing on the threshold. I took an involuntary step in her direction, feeling...joy?...at the fact that I had not killed her.

"Aislyn." I breathed. She flinched away from me and it hurt somehow. "Are you all right?" I found myself asking.

"No." she answered. "I mean, they patched me up and gave me a transfusion and everything...but they lied to me."

"Gods in their heavens collide!" Darrin exploded. "They lied to you as well?! Who haven't they lied to!?"

"Judah," Aislyn ignored Darrin's ranting, "do you know anything about what is happening to us? I went to see the witch. She told me the angels have been soul-siphoning us. What's going on?"

I sighed. There was a good reason that the demon was enraged. The things Josephine had been coerced into revealing had shocked us both.

"We've been played." I informed the wolf. "Every single one of us, from the beginning."

"Played?" her eyebrows lifted.

"Fate Path doesn't call for a Messiah." Darrin broke the news.

The mutt glanced from me to the demon and her face paled further. "What?"

"This isn't written in destiny." I continued the explanation. "We are caught up in angelic scheme."

"What is it with you immortals!" she shouted, glaring from me to Darrin with flashing, luminous eyes. "You take an eternity to explain anything! I don't freakin' have forever! So one of you had better tell me something, or so help me I will snap your necks!"

Darrin glowered at me. "Fine." I huffed. "Aislyn, sit down." she did as I asked. "We've been had," I began explaining. "The angels never intended to give us anything without getting something in return. And they wanted more than the witch or the elf in custody. They wanted pieces of our souls. Yours, mind, the elf's, and the witch's."

Her amber eyes went wide. "I know that already. The question is *why*, Judah."

"Isn't that the million lifetime question?" Darrin grouched.

"The angels want their independence from Fate Path." I ignored him. "They are tired of being the second class citizens of the world, chained to the beck and call of a God who is often silent. They want their independence, their final freedom, and they believe they have found a way."

"Why couldn't they just fall?" she asked. "Wouldn't becoming a demon..."

"It doesn't work that way." Darrin explained, his tone gentle. "Falling doesn't change an angel's destiny. It simply flips a coin. One side to the other. We demons are still bound to Fate Path as much as the angels. Neither race has free will...both of us are chained to the edicts of God."

"And the angels want free will?" Aislyn asked. "Like humans?"

"Yes." Darrintek answered. "They long for it. For as long as humans have existed, angels have envied them, for they are the cherished children of God."

"So why do they want us?" Aislyn asked. "What do we have that the angels need?"

"Souls." I replied. "The angels are taking bits and pieces of ours, hoping that if they fit them together and unite them, they will have what they most desire."

"And that is?" Aislyn's voice trembled.

"A human soul." I answered. "They want to make a human soul."

My lips are brass and my tongue is fire. I am afraid to speak lest I melt my words; lest I lose control in front of you. So long have I waited for this moment that brings me to my knees.

The Eyes of Eternity sought you out from the beginning, watched as your childhood was drenched with blood. It should never have touched your hands. Why did it touch your hands?

For so long, I have loved as was forbidden. But now, face to face, I desire my freedom more than ever. But you, you are my reason and the key.

You said your heart belongs to another. But they cannot give you the world. Do you not desire more than what your existence has granted you? Is that not what defines a human life?

A Different Sort of Hell – Kieran

She loves me. That thought had repeated in my brain at least a hundred thousand times. *I never in all my years imagined this day.* Icy pain fissured through my lungs. *My dream and my life reaching their fulfillment.*

I took in my surroundings. The angels had taken me to a room, an interrogation room. Stainless steel table, centrifugal lighting, monochromatic walls. I felt comforted by the fact that I was seated on one side of the table, not lying on and chained to it. A vision of pure beauty entered the room, the scarlet-haired, silver-eyed angel who had torn me away from Mia.

*The witch. **My** witch. A woman who loves me…a woman who has shown me that the world can change. A woman I can—do— love.*

"Are you well, Kieran Shandera?" asked a voice made of purple silk and stained glass.

I looked up, staring into brilliant eyes. "No." I answered, telling all the truth. "But I am certain you realize this."

She sat down, looking worn, in pain…almost human. "The torture was not my idea, Ms. Shandera."

"Call me Kieran." I bit. "I believe we know each other well enough for that."

"I am the Secretary of Angelic Affairs." she would not meet my eyes. "But my name is Josephine. You may call me as such."

"Josephine." I laugh-coughed. "So you aren't responsible for…" I started coughing and doubled over, trying to even out my breathing. I held up my hand, showing the Secretary of Angelic Affairs my blood, "…this?"

The angel paled. "What on Earth?"

"Hell, actually." I quipped. "Where you *locked* me in a dream and had me *tortured*…only to wake and find it real."

"The effects would not have translated if you had simply revealed the truth! Delving into your memories was the simplest way of...of reaching you."

"Had you seen into my memories, you would have known I would reveal nothing." I stated, wondering why Josephine seemed very ill at ease.

"Yes." she sighed. "Alas, contracted work does allow for a larger margin of error, and for that I apologize."

"You did not even have the decency to rape my mind yourself?" I shook my head.

"I didn't want to harm you." Josephine almost whispered, sending shock through my veins. "I only wanted the truth of who killed our seraphim."

"You could have asked." I said. "You have the greatest power in Heaven, second to God himself. You could have found me, and asked. I would not have lied to you. I am not lying to you now."

"I know." she buried her head in...shame? Could angels feel shame? "There is no way I can apologize. But...but there is a reason you are here."

"I killed the angel." I answered. "With my knife. Your angels confiscated it when they took me prisoner. You'll find blood still on it." I extended my right hand and showed her the burns. "You can see where its blood marked me. I killed an angel to protect myself and my friend. That's why I am here, at least. To face Heaven's justice...to pay with my soul, if I am not mistaken."

Josephine rose and began pacing the room, wings bristling with agitation. *I have never thought an angel would act so...human.*

"I wanted it to be the witch!" she erupted, startling me. "It should have been her! Then my seraphim would be alive, and you wouldn't be in this mess!"

Confusion riddled me like bullets. "Why do you care?" I asked. "Why do you care what happens to me?"

Josephine glared at me, looking as though I had slapped her across the face. "How can you ask that?" she threw another from left field. "Kieran, I love you!"

They'd kept her way too long. I paced thah floor like a caged animal. Blood was screamin' through my veins, cryin' to be released. It was thah powah that had torn a hole in Heaven. If I had to use it to save her, I'd spill every last drop I had.

"Calm down, little witch." a cool voice cautioned.

I turned lightnin' quick an' saw thah vamp, thah wolf, an' thah demon standin' theah. One person missin'.

My elf. Please, Kieran, please be okay.

"Whaddaya want?"

Wolf girl took a step forwahd, sensin' my agitation an' probably smellin' my fear. "We know what's going on." she said, an' my eahs pricked up.

"What?"

"The soul-shards the angels have been stealing? They want to combine them; they're trying to make a human soul."

I felt like a piano had fallen from thah sky an' turned what little brain I had left intah jello. "Why thah fuck do they want a human soul?" I asked.

"Free will." thah demon explained. "Only humans have true free will in the Eyes of Eternity. Vampires, werewolves, witches, and elves are hybrid races, bound by curses and bloodlines. A mixture, if you will, of the divine and the beloved."

"Ahn't thah divine an' thah beloved thah same thing?" I asked, wonderin' what thah hell I was stuck in this time. *An' wheah is Kieran?*

118

"No." Judah broke in. "Of all the races, only the humans were given complete freedom of choice. They are the only race to walk outside the lines set by Fate Path."

"An' thah angels want that." I said, stahtin' to feel less hungovah. "An' they're tryin' to do what? Ordah a three soul combo meal?"

"Three?" Aislyn questioned the demon.

Darrintek shook his head. "According to Josephine's calculations, they would need four pieces, one from each race, to complete the human soul.

Werewolves and witches, both once human and turned by magic, one race by force, the other by choice. Their souls are still largely human, and the component of magic merely sweetens the deal.

Next they need the piece of a vampire and elf, one race the children of demons and humans, the other of angels and humans. Elves and vampires have the immortal qualities the angels would not wish to relinquish. And both races provide the capacity for good and evil."

"Fuckin' angels!" I swore. "Mahchin' into all our lives an' screwin' 'em up thah ass with a rubbah mallet. But you're tellin' me that elves and vamps were made by demons an angels gettin' freaky with humans?"

Thah demon laughed his ass off 'til I glared him intah shuttin' thah hell up. "Yes." he said. "Vampires are the bastard children of the angels. They are sickening reminders that angels once found humans beautiful and desirable. Why do you think they were banned from heaven? We demons take credit for the elves."

Elves...Kieran. Holy shit! They need an elven soul! She had that lettah from thah Depahtment of Angelic Affaihs! Fuck me!

"Kieran." I whispahed thah name. All three of thah othahs stared at me. "Thah angels took Kieran." I explained. "She's thah last ingredient in their damn soul cocktail."

Aislyn looked to Judah. "We have to find her before the angels soul-siphon her."

"An' how do ya suppose we do that!" I yelled. "Ask an' angel to borrow a phone an' call in a fuckin' aih strike?"

Thah vamp smiled like he knew my innahmost thoughts. "It's far simpler actually." he tapped his nose. "We follow the smell of elven blood."

I threw up my hands in despaih. "Oh, this is just depressin'."

Love of a Broken God – Kieran

The room smeared to a thousand shades of horror. Fear gripped my heart and constricted my lungs until I had to cough to breathe. The taste of copper filled my mouth and I spat blood onto the table. Josephine winced as she sat down and buried her face in her hands.

"This is not at all what I had planned." she said, looking at me with sparks in her eyes. "I sent you an invitation. You were meant to come straight to me, as a guest of Heaven, not a prisoner."

"You love me?" I asked, incredulous. "You had me hunted, tried to assassinate me, and then had me thrown back into the hell of torture. What part of that looks like love?"

She slammed her fist onto the table. "I had no *choice!*" she shouted. "I. Am. An. Angel! There are *protocols* I am forced to follow! I am *not permitted to* **love***!*"

Glittering tears streamed from radiant eyes. But the hope in the silver did not grip my heart as fiercely as the love in my witch's blue.

"So why have you brought me to this place?" I asked.

"I was building a world for you." she whispered. The secretarial bureaucrat façade fell away. All I saw now was a beautiful woman in chains. "I've watched you, Kieran, as only angels can. I saw you born, and grow, and bury your father…and take his place in the elven armies to spare your younger brother. I witnessed your kindness and your mercy, your brilliance and your hope and I…I cried as I watched you tortured; I sang as I watched you heal, and I began to plan a universe where we could be together."

"You are an angel." I breathed, stunned all over again. "Angels do not feel love."

She laughed; a tortured, demented sound. "That is what the centuries have schooled all races into believing. We are the first creations of a cruel god, Kieran, gifted with all the feelings of humans, but the inability to act on them."

"Ancestors preserve us." I quoted my mother. "So what is this plan, Josephine? What do you want?"

"I want you to love me. I want to heal you; give you back everything that was stolen from you in the war. I want to love you."

"But you can't."

She hung her head, remorseful. "I have a plan."

"What does it have to do with soul-siphoning?" I asked, wanting the shock to end and the answer to come into the light.

The angel paled. "What?"

"Mia. Aislyn. Judah." I said their names, staring through her. "A witch, a werewolf, and a vampire. You've stolen pieces of their souls. Why? What do you need them for?"

"They are my gift to you."

I stood, ignoring the pain. I felt sick, and not from the grating of my broken ribs or the blood coating my teeth. "What sort of horrific gift is this?"

"The gift of an angel's life." she rose, walked to me, and laid her hands on my shoulders. "I am constructing a human soul. So that I might have free will. So that I might leave this damned eternity and be free to love you."

"Goddess." I pulled away from the angel's touch. Bile rose in my throat. "How could you justify this? You've soul-siphoned three people, three *innocent* people who will spend the rest of their lives as only half of themselves."

I shook my head, unable to countenance the depravity it would take to stoop to such depths.

Josephine's countenance darkened. "Four."

"What?"

"Four souls. Four corners of the earth. The siphoning is not yet complete."

"The fourth soul is elven." I hissed, feeling rage come to the forefront. "Isn't it, Josephine? How many more people will you kill?"

"I haven't killed anyone." Josephine defended herself.

"A soul is someone's connection...the link to the All that Is." I ranted. "I've had it ripped, torn, shredded. It is the worst form of murder, Secretary. What you've done is..."

"People do the unthinkable for love." Josephine said. "I see it every day."

"If you love me," I pleaded, "take me to the elf. What you're doing—it's horrible, and painful. I know I can help them. Please, do this. For me."

I saw resignation and reluctance in her eyes. She clapped her hands and the wall turned transparent. I looked through my new window and saw an elf strapped to a chair, hooked to wires and tubes and IVs. She had long black hair, and pale skin like mine. Her face lifted, hair fell aside, and eyes looked into mine, pained and green.

"Reya." I breathed, touching the window. I looked back at the angel, filled with a new sort of fury. "You fucked up, goddamn, celestial butcher." I borrowed words from Mia's vocabulary. "Take me to my sister. Do it now."

The guilt-stricken Secretary of Angelic Affairs waved her hand and the wall fell away. I rushed to my sister; her anguished eyes welled with tears. She reached out and touched my face, her fingers grazing the trail of blood at the corner of my mouth.

"Kieran," she whispered, "you're bleeding."

My heart broke.

Heaven Falls from Grace – Judah

Eternity is shaking, crumbling at the edges. I can taste the fragments as equations splinter; feel the crackling in the air. Time itself is grasping at control. And losing.

"What thah hell ah we even lookin' for?" the witch asked. She had joined us in our quest, in our hatred of heaven.

"For the elf." the mutt...Aislyn...answered. "If we can keep the angels from taking her soul, we have a chance at winning this."

Her words were so hopeful...so mortal. "Winning what?" I asked Darrintek. "We are three broken creatures. How can we hope to stand against Heaven? And Fate Path? What does destiny mandate?"

The demon's face turned grim. "If we cannot think of some way to stop them, Fate Path won't matter anymore. It's unraveling as it is. The equation is almost completely destabilized."

"An' thah cryptics ain't helpin' nothin'!" the witch yelled.

"Angels with free will finally be allowed to release their millennia ancient rage on humankind. We don't stop it, that's what happens. Apocalypse. End of Days. Ragnarok. I am a demon. I enjoy my identity. And Fate Path. But the angels are not like us...they have lost their taste for our cold war."

"It was an angel who sought to dethrone God." I reminded the other two.

"An' now they wanna give it anothah try." Mia spat. "Fuck them an' their show. Tek, do ya have any idea what we're even lookin' for?"

"The holiest place in Heaven." Darrin answered. "I cannot set foot there and I cannot aid you in this battle. I must return to my domain. May God grant you grace."

We all fell silent at the demon's words. Darrintek cut a hole in the atmosphere and prepared to step through it.

"Judah, I hope you can forgive me." he said. "I never thought they would lie."

"I never thought a demon would be more honest than an angel." Ailsyn said. "I will...miss you, Darrin."

He smiled. "Don't fight your nature, wolf. You took life in defense of life, not out of malicious intent, and it is a shame that your people are too shortsighted to understand such a thing. But God is more forgiving of the past than men or angels.

Judah, you are not a monster. Believe me, for I know the definition. Witch," he turned his violet eyes to Mia, "love conquers everything. Even mortality. The day you forget that is the day you die."

With that, my friend stepped through the wall between the worlds. I turned to Mia.

"What did he mean?"

Her eyes were tortured; her voice non-chalant. "Hell if I know. Let's get to this Holy of Holies, though. Kieran's in trouble."

"Where is this place?" Aislyn asked, looking down the golden streets.

"The place that is prepared." I answered, feeling instinct tug at my veins. "The seat of God when he returns to the world. New Jerusalem. The heart of Heaven."

I am a guardian of peace and light. I have striven for centuries to follow the path set for me. And life has continued as life will in Heaven. Endless monotony.

I am forced to watch love; forced to watch humans dance in sick mimicry of emotion, not realizing that those who are closest to God would kill for what they have.

And I have. Not to my own eyes, but to another's. But humans have always killed for love. What is it that they named it? A crime of passion?

Am I now a criminal?

The Salvation Clause – Kieran

I shot the angel a glare of pure wrath. *My sister!* my thoughts screamed. *She has **nothing** to do with this! She was not in the witch wars and she is independent of the schemes of heaven!*

"Reya," I whispered, touching her face. Her skin was shockingly cold. "Honey, look at me." her eyes fluttered closed, and did not open. "Come on, baby, open your eyes."

"There is nothing you can do, Kieran." Josephine stood behind me. "She gave her soul over willingly."

I stood, shaking. "What lie did you tell her?" I demanded. "That's my little sister, you selfish whore! She had *nothing* to do with this! What the hell did you tell her!?"

Josephine turned away, yet another who would not meet my gaze. "We told her it was for you." the Secretary admitted. "We told her that it would help you heal."

Tears of rage poured down and my lungs *screamed* as I breathed deep. "God. Damn. You." my voice quavered. "God damn you! How can you claim you are no murderer!?"

Noises drew my attention from the angel I wanted to kill. It if was more angels, I would kill them all, with my bare hands if need be. The door to the room burst open and three figures flooded in.

"So this is thah cornahstone of heaven?" a familiar voice asked and light filled my heart.

"Is nothing sacred anymore?" Josephine questioned. "Is every door in Heaven splayed open for voyeurs?"

"Shut up." I ordered. "And don't even *think* of using angelsong. I will kill you myself."

The Secretary fell silent and I saw sorrow, true anguish, in her face. *To never be able to love,* my gentler heart took over. *To be bound and chained to something so much greater than yourself, unable to move or change, yet able to feel, to long…to desire. I never thought I could feel hatred and pity equally co-mingle.*

Mia ran over to me, worry lighting her divine blue eyes. "Kieran, ah you okay? Has she done anythin' to you?"

"I'm okay." I lied for her sake. Rage and mercy warred in my veins, burning me alive.

"Kieran?" my sister's voice. My mind swirled as it tore in a thousand directions. I spoke to Mia with my eyes, begging her to let me tear myself away. She nodded and I ran to Reya's side.

"Hey, honey." I whispered, brushing her hair back from her face. "Are you all right? Are you in pain?"

"No pain." she breathed. "But I don't feel right. Where...where am I?"

"You're in heaven."

"I'm dead?" her green eyes went wide.

"No, baby, no. You're not dead. You were tricked by the angels." I looked up to hide my tears; found Josephine's silver eyes staring through me. "What did you do to her?" I asked. "I want to know everything."

"It's called the salvation clause." Josephine informed us. "That one rare variable in the life equation where someone gives their soul for another."

"And if that person is deceived?" I asked. "If the salvation clause is invoked to blackmail someone into relinquishing a piece of their soul?"

Josephine's face hardened. "It's called good politics."

"You bitch." I hissed. "You won't suffer from this at all?"

"I will profit from it." her voice turned to ice. "As will you, Kieran Shandera. I will give you Heaven, earth...even hell if you want."

"Kieran, what thah *fuck* is goin' on?" Mia asked.

"The world is about to change." Josephine addressed the group. "You are here at the turning point of Heaven. Fate Path is about to be destroyed."

"Oh my God." the werewolf breathed.

Josephine snapped her head towards the wolf. "God is dead."

The World's Ending – Aislyn

The elf didn't look happy and she reeked of anger and anxiety. My vampire growled, and the witch just seemed pissed off.

*God is dead…*the words reverberated in my ears. Wolf yipped and howled in protest.

"If ever there was a moment for a Messiah to appear," Judah whispered, "this would be it."

I felt so hopeless, so powerless before it all. I came from a line of warriors; power lost to time coursed through my veins, and I could do nothing. The one who could was dying already.

"What now, Josephine?" Kieran asked. "After you kill God, then what? Are you so desperate to know love that you will damn an entire world?"

"Haven't you seen enough?" Josephine questioned, examining each one of us as though we held the answers. "You revel all day in freedoms you never *think* of us not having."

"But why do we gotta pay?" Mia asked. "What did thah four of us do to get Heaven pissed off at us?"

Josephine smiled, but it was manic, deranged. "You were the ones no one would miss." she flicked her eyes at each of us in turn. "Judah, the vampire who longs for his humanity. Mia, the witch sentenced to death by her own coven. Aislyn, the werewolf who would be executed, were her crimes ever discovered, and who despises her own cursed existence."

"And Reya," Kieran's voice whipped through the air, "an elven girl, attached to no war, no army, nothing. Why did you take her, Josephine!? Why my sister!?"

Silence fell like a shroud over the entire scene. Mia broke it.

"What thah fuck!" she exclaimed. "Kieran, I thought they were aftah your soul!"

The elf coughed and wiped blood from her lips. "I thought so too." she said. "And it would be better if they *had* taken my soul. Then," she glared at Josephine, "you might have known forgiveness."

"Shut up, elf!" the mentally unstable Secretary shouted. "You have no concept of what we have endured! The angels are a race enslaved by the hand of a cruel god! All we want is *our freedom!*"

Metallic beeping keened through the room and Josephine's face lit up.

"It's time." she said, and the room went pale. "Time for destiny to unravel and for God on this throne to shed tears of remorse. By uniting four elements, four souls, I will create the beloved of the Most High. I will be the favored child of heaven. And," she looked at Kieran, "*you **will** love me.*"

"Oh, deah sacred heaven!" Mia groaned. "I'm in hell."

"What do you think the world is soon to become?" Judah asked. "Welcome to the future, Mia."

Inside, my bones shook, and wolf howled as though her heart, and mine, would break.

No Greater Love – Kieran

The world was ending and all I could feel was pity. Pity for the furious angel who claimed she loved me; who held the fragments of four souls in her hands.

An angel free from Fate Path who believes that all she desires is love. The chairman at God's right hand crying herself to sleep at night. I will show her what love is. I have to, to prove to her that the world is still worth saving. I believe that with my very…soul.

I knelt beside my sister and smiled, trying to comfort her. "Reya," I held her face in my hands and stared into her eyes, "I love you. Don't ever forget that. You hear me?"

Fear crept into her hazy eyes. "Kieran, what are you doing?"

"Changing the world." I said, hoping it would be true. "Tell mom I love her."

"Kieran, don't…" my baby sister begged, but I turned a deaf ear. My heart was screaming loud enough.

"Kieran," Mia ran up to me, "what thah fuck ah you thinkin'?"

I looked at the witch, the sister of my torturer, the one woman who had proved my beliefs, hard fought for and desperately clung to, had merit. She had softened the blow of a mortal life. I loved her.

"Mia," I pulled her into my arms and whispered into her ear, "I love you. I want to spend the rest of my life learning you, changing the world with you. But that's my little sister…and Josephine has taken a piece of her soul."

Mia drew away and both of us heard Josephine begin a bone-rattling chant in angelsong. "I undahstand." she said, choking up. "You gotta give it all for family. Just come back to me, Kieran."

I can't. "I love you, Mia." I said the words again. "Make sure Reya gets home safe…for me. Our mother worries."

Mia's eyes went wide. "What thah...Kieran, what ah you doin'?"

The unthinkable. "I love you."

I turned away from her and walked toward Josephine. The vampire caught my eyes and nodded. Aislyn looked between the two of us and whispered to Judah. When I saw her eyes again, they were filled with tears. I swallowed down my own.

It's better this way. I reasoned with myself. *If not now, I would soon be dead from the angel's torture. At least this way,* I glanced back one last time on Mia, *I'll be able to fix it. For them.*

"Josephine." I spoke as loud as I could without coughing.

It broke her concentration and she turned to me, wings bristling. Her eyes were wide, glowing, fierce. She looked more like a demon than an angel.

"What do you want?" she asked, venom in her voice.

"To show you what love is." I told her, feeling my heart hammer against my ribs. "You're going about this all wrong, Madame Secretary. Love isn't selfish. It doesn't use others to meet its own ends."

"Well then what do you suggest I do?" she challenged. "I have no options left to me."

"Yes, you do." I swallowed down fear and regret. "I'm giving you a way free. I'm invoking the salvation clause."

"Kieran, no!" Reya screamed.

"You're what?" the angel recoiled.

"The rare variable in the life equation when one person gives up their soul for another." I answered. "Give them back what you stole from them." I gestured to the victims around me, the man and women who had suffered for this angel's misguided belief that she loved...me. "And take mine in their place."

Josephine started laughing. "Is it any wonder I love you?" she asked. "So beautiful, so brave. But your soul won't do. You are elven. You are immortal, and therefore bound to Fate Path."

"You weren't watching me as closely as you said then." I revealed it all. "Or you would know that the witches stole my immortality. I *killed* an angel. Fate Path has no hold on me. Take the offer. Follow your law, Madame Secretary. I, Kieran Shandera, invoke the salvation clause."

The room fell silent in shock. Mia's blue eyes filled with tears.

"But in order to do that, you will have to…" Josephine stammered, "I cannot take your soul. You'll die."

I walked in close to her. "Look into my eyes." I said, tasting my last words. "Believe me."

She wore a knife at her belt, and I closed my hand around it.

"I do not know," I spoke, for her ears alone, "the extent of the Grand Design, or Fate Path, or what sort of God would burden any one race with what the angels endure. But I know what love is. And I am going to complete your dream. My soul," I slid the knife from its sheath, "is yours."

I plunged the blade into my stomach, pulled it out and threw it at Josephine's feet. My legs went numb and I crumpled to the floor, feeling the wound in my body as my last testament. Blood bubbled over my lips. I had chosen a slow death. I wanted to savor my life as it ended; as I gave it for love.

True Immortality – Judah

The scent of blood filled the room. The elf fell to the floor, clutching the wound in her gut.

"Judah," Aislyn pressed herself against me and I wrapped an arm about her, "what is she doing?"

Had I possessed all my soul, it would have been crushed. "One for the many." I breathed. "The scapegoat. The purest given in place of the defiled."

"But why?" the wolf asked. Her tears soaked into my shirt.

I have lived centuries praying for this day, never expecting it to come to pass. Never expecting. "For love." the words left my lips. They felt holy, sacred.

"No other reason?" Aislyn whispered. "None at all?"

"No other reason."

A wail shattered the holiness of that moment. My gaze lifted and I saw Josephine go to her knees.

Even angels bow before this, my detached conscious smiled. *God himself should be weeping on his throne.*

"Kieran," Josephine groaned in angelsong. I had only ever heard that voice used to command; never to grieve. The beauty broke my heart. "Is this love?" the angel asked. "Is this, in the end, what it means? Vampire, you have seen much of the world. Tell me what this," she held up her hand, stained with Kieran's blood, "means!"

"That is godhood." I said, holding Aislyn tighter as she wept. "That is an act befitting the Messiah you claim does not exist. I suggest you honor the deal she brokered, Madame Secretary. Return what was taken."

"Not until she dies." Josephine's tears glittered like diamonds.

"Do it now." Kierna's blood-soaked voice. "While I live."

Josephine bowed her head. "Perhaps God is not so cruel to us." I alone heard her voice. She spoke again, louder. "Your souls are returned to you."

Stillness electrified the air and the hair on the back of my neck rose. Peace infused me as I felt something fit together, as I felt disease flow out of my veins, as the chance to live centuries departed. My soul was my own again, my mortality had been returned.

But at what cost do my dreams come to their fruition? At what cost? A pure soul for that of a demon. The equation is set aright. All is well in this world. Except...

"Fuck. This. Shit." Mia, the strongest voice of any of us.

She rushed to Kieran and shoved Josephine out of the way. The breaking angel did not resist. "This ain't hapennin'." Mia prayed, pressing her hand over Kieran's wound. "I won't let them make ya a mahtyr. Stay with me, Kieran."

"It's useless, isn't it?" Aislyn asked, afraid to hope.

A tear crept from my eye for the first time in two hundred years. "I'm afraid it is."

"What do we do?" Aislyn's voice turned to steel and the wolf's eyes shone through. "You're human again. You could kill that secretary bitch."

"No." I shook my head, gazing at the miserable tableau of the witch and the elf. "We do what Kieran would do."

"And what is that?" Aislyn demanded.

"Forgive them."

Theah was so much blood. It was everywheah, on my hands, my face, thah floor.

"M...Mia?" Kieran spoke and more blood frothed between her lips.

"Don't talk." I urged, forcin' magic intah her body, tryin' to keep her heart beatin'. Deah God, theah was too much blood. She didn't have much more to lose.

Thah aih stahted to smell like cinnamon. Sweat ran down my forehead and trickled intah my eyes.

"Let...let it go." Kieran choked. "Let me go."

"Can't do that, babe." I tried to smile. "Love don't let go. I learned that from you."

"So...beautiful." she grinned, an' those lovely black eyes went distant.

Her skin was pasty white an' thah edges of her lips had a bluish tinge.

This ain't good.

"Kieran." I tapped her cheek as her eyes fluttahed closed. "Kieran, stay with me, baby. Don't you go dyin' on me now. Not aftah all we've been through."

"Give it up, witch." Josephine groaned. "Let her have her honorable death."

"Fuck you!" I yelled, putting more preshah on thah wound, though I knew it was useless. "I won't let her die just so you can get ya Christmas wish."

Kieran's body stahted shakin' an' I stopped thah flow of magic. Regulah stuff was pointless. Teahs welled in my eyes an' spilled ovah.

"Fuck you, Kieran." I sobbed. "Why thah hell ah you doin' this? What thah **fuck** were you thinkin'?"

Thah world went quiet when Kieran stopped breathin'. "Baby, don't go." I pleaded, holdin' her close to me. "Don't go...please don't go."

"It seems somehow painful, holding your dream." Josephine's monotone broke through.

I looked at her, watched her hold thah soul of thah woman I loved. "Ya fuckin' think?"

"Do you love her too?"

"Yeah." I admitted.

"Then how can you endure watching her die?"

"'Cause of what she's dyin' for." my voice cracked. "What's with thah inquisition? Just take your soul an' go. Live ya fuckin' life, but don't you **evah** forget what one war-scarred elf who could'a lived a justahfied life of hate did for you and your damned angels."

"I cannot." Josephine said, letting thah soul fly loose from her fingahtips. "I cannot have faith in a world where love makes death a gift. I am sorry that the only thing I can give her is a soul at rest. Forgive me, Mia."

I laid Kieran back down on thah ground, a mad scheme wormin' intah my brain. *Death as a gift. Thah outpourin' of blood.*

"Hang in theah." I kissed Kieran's forehead. "It ain't quittin' time yet."

I grabbed Josephine's knife. This would need more than I'd evah given, even for my brothah. I placed thah tip of the angel's blade on my palm, slashing it across with a quick jerk.

"You ridiculous little witch." Josephine intoned. "You cannot bring back the dead. If death is love's greatest gift, then love **cannot** bring back the dead!"

"Buy ya'self a fuckin' clue." I snapped.

I pressed my bloody palm to the gapin' hole in Kieran's gut, reaching deep intah my magic and forcing it from my blood and into her own, driving the life through her veins, forcing her heart to re-staht from thah preshah.

I glared at Josephine. "If she comes back," I panted, stahtin' to feel dizzy, "ya give up ya fuckin' soul stealin' schemes. Ah we cleah?"

"I no longer desire those things." Josephine lifted her knife and cradled it to her. "Love is not as I thought it."

I laughed 'cause I was insane an' 'cause thah angel was stahtin' to make sense. "Ya nevah figured for thah pain, did ya?"

"I never imagined this...nightmare...would be caused by love. What did you do to her?"

My vision was tuhnin' to shocky static mode, but I kept forcing magic into Kieran's body, felt our blood tie in togethah, felt my heart skip a beat as hers stahted pumpin' blood again.

"Gave her my blood." I answahed thah angel. "Half my life. My heart's beatin' for both of us now."

"And what makes you sacrifice this?"

"Love." it was thah only thing that mattahed.

"Love." she smirked, starin' at that blood all ovah thah place. "I cannot think of it as anything but a disease."

I smiled, lookin' down at my elf. Her eyelids twitched. I put my eah to her nose an' felt thah warmth of her breath. Joy struck like lightnin' through my system an' teahs of somethin' greatah than grief took ovah. I turned back to thah angel who had put me through hell.

"You've had an epiphany. Congratu-fuckin'-lations."

The sky is broken; the world rent asunder in shades of scarlet. I have seen the sum of my desires, seen them bleed out in front of me. I have dreamt enough. I have dreamt too far. Hope is the sin of angels.

Love—Death—Pain—all as one. All are One. Perhaps they are not the beloved of God. Perhaps they are his playthings; Earth the Coliseum in which the Most High holds his blood sports. Love is nothing more than a tool used to kill. It is a cancer and a uselessness. There is a reason that our world has been ordered. Everything to its purpose and its place.

Already I stand above the earth. I stand at the right hand of the Father. And if God is Love, then God is Death. What I feel is the desire, not to love, but to show love. I will become the hand of God. I will bring death. But I am an angel. I cannot kill.

Father, forgive me. I know full well what I do. So does the world unturn.

So now I fall from Heaven.

Away from the Light – Kieran

An obsidian bench stands before an entryway. Light streams from behind the door in welcome, but I do not go to it. I sit down on the bench and wait. For what, I do not know.

The door opens without a sound and a familiar face emerges. Scarlet hair and...violet?...eyes.

"You're allowed to go in." *Josephine gestures towards the light.* "You are all the rage of Heaven."

"And you?" *I ask, feeling concern.* "Where will you go?"

"I signed my resignation this morning." *she admits.* "There is no joy left for me in Heaven."

"So you're falling?" *I inquire as sorrow washes over me.*

"Yes. I have sat in the seat of power for too long. It is past time to abdicate." *she laughs.* "Perhaps a darker set of chains will suit me."

"You could have had your freedom." *I say.* "I gave you my soul. Why did you return it?"

"Because I never could accept the gift of death; of you taking on the burden of my existence. You broke me, Kieran. You shattered me with a definition of love I did not see...and now I do not wish to see it."

"Why?"

"An angel is not permitted to take life, and it is rare that we ever die. Love must not include death. Love is undying."

"Love is the sum of the All that Is." *I say, feeling pity once again.* "It is not attached to a life. It is life."

"You have far more faith than even I, who have stood face to face with the Creator."

"Do angels even need faith?" *I question.* "You see all of Earth and all of Heaven. Why do you speak of faith?"

Surprise lights her unnatural eyes. Demon's eyes. "I cannot answer you. There are things in Heaven and Earth that surpass my knowledge." *she sighs.* "I would have loved you, Kieran. I would have given you the world."

"Good-bye, Josephine." I say, watching her turn from me. "I hope you find love in its true form."

"I did." she smiles. "I found you. They will welcome you in Heaven, Kieran. You can have a life free from the suffering of love."

"Am I dead?"

"Not yet." Josephine shakes her head in disbelief. "The witch keeps your heart beating with her own. Why she would endanger her life to save yours is beyond me."

"Sometimes living isn't so important." I smile, my thoughts turning to Mia. **She's alive. Thank God.** "I would know."

Her hand reaches out and caresses my cheek. "My beautiful immortal. We should have been forever." she sighs. "Farewell, my darling."

Josephine departs from heaven, to what end, I do not know.

I turn to the door, the light and the warmth it holds behind it. **A life free, I think, no more hurt, no more sorrow. Peace at last, no war-torn world. I chose death. Why...why not embrace it? Why return?**

My mother's image invades my mind, followed by Reya's...and...hers. My witch. My love. My blue-eyed hope.

Why return to suffering?

"Love." I answer my own question. **The same reason I left.**

I turn my back to the door.

Heaven can wait...a little longer.

The Changing World — Mia

If theah is a God in Heaven, heah me now. Don't let her die. Please. I've done all I can. Can't go no furthah on this one.

I paced thah hospital floor, hatin' that I was theah, hatin' thah smell, an' hatin' thah fact that no doctah would talk to me.

Blood magic only did so much; it couldn't fix all thah damage done to Kieran's body. That's why aftah thah angels booted us out, I'd gone straight heah, to anothah version of hell.

I cradled my bandaged hand against my chest, hopin' for thah millionth fuckin' time that it had been enough. Enough blood, enough powah...enough to keep her alive.

I collapsed intah one of thah crappy plastic chaihs an' ran my good hand through my hair. Reya was somewheah in thah back, bein' treated for dehydration an' exhaustion. I was on thah brink of complete breakdown myself, but I couldn't let go just yet.

Gotta keep holdin' on...for her sake.

Thah doors whooshed open an' a woman rushed through them, lookin' all around. She brushed her hair behind her eahs. They were pointy. I swallowed hahd, knowin' that this was gonna be difficult.

"Ms. Shandera?" I asked, walkin' towahds her. She perked up an' looked at me, confused. Her snappin' black eyes looked so much like Kieran's that I stahted smilin'.

"Who...who are you?" she asked.

I swallowed again. Kieran was thah only elf I'd evah met who wanted to keep the peace. If an elf could get a witch in a dahk alley an' slaughtah 'em, they would do it in a heartbeat.

I extended my hand. "My name is Mia Redblade." I introduced myself. "I brought your daughtahs in."

Her grip on my hand faltahed, fell away. "Redblade?" she slanted her eyes at me. "That's...that's a witch name."

Heah it comes. "Yes, ma'am. Your daughtah saved my life."

I saw angah rise an' fall in her face. "At this moment, I could care less." she tried to smile. "I thought both my daughters were lost to me, but now I can celebrate instead of mourn. If I owe that debt to a witch, it is one I will gladly bear."

She sounds like Kieran. I smiled, feelin' relief wash ovah me. *An immortal life with a loving family, guilt nagged at my thoughts, that's what my people took from Kieran. No wondah hate runs so deep in thah blood.*

"Mom?"

Both of us looked up an' saw Reya in thah waitin' room. She had a bit more color in her cheeks, but her eyes were exhausted an' she looked unsteady on her feet.

I smiled as thah two ran to each othah an' embraced, both cryin' teahs of pure joy an' relief.

"I was so worried." Ms. Shandera examined her daughtah from head to toe, with such love in her eyes it almost broke my heart.

"I'm okay, mom." Reya soothed her. "I'll tell you everything. But first, mom, this is Mia. Mia, this is my mother, Eryn."

"We've met." Eryn wouldn't look at me. "Reya, where is Kieran? Is she all right? They wouldn't tell me anything over the phone."

Reya's face fell an' Eryn went pale.

Fuck me. They're relivin' a horrah that no one should go through even once.

"They took her intah surgery 'bout an hour ago." I spoke when neithah of them did. "I haven't seen thah doctah yet."

Thah fury came back in Eryn's face. "What the hell did you do to my daughter, witch!? Haven't your kind done enough to my family!? Can't you let this war die!?"

Her hands grabbed hold of my shouldahs an' she shook em, beatin' my collahbones with her fists.

"Hasn't she been hurt enough!?" Eryn sobbed. "How much blood will it take to sate your thirst!?"

Her words tore intah my heart like a razah blade.

"I'm sohry." I whispahd, wrappin' my arms around her as her blows turned to desperate clinging. "I'm sohry for what my people did to ya fam'ly an' ya daughtah. But please undahstand, I want this war dead as much as you do. Kieran means thah world to me."

She's my everythin'.

"You're sorry?" Eryn asked, traces of old poison in her voice. "*You're* sorry? The witch wars took my husband! The witch wars threw my daughter on my doorstep half-dead! And when the treaty was signed, I thought it was

146

ended, I thought it was *safe*! Now I find my daughter on death's door once again with a witch in a waiting room telling me that she's **sorry!?**"

I bowed my head. "I nevah raised a blade in thah battles. I nevah undahstood what hatin' thah elves did for my people. Thah witches wanted to kill me, Ms. Eryn. I got thah shahp end of thah sword, but that don't mean they liked me. I got no love left for my people. I ain't on some re-staht thah war crusade. I just wanna make sure Kieran's gonna be okay."

"She would be *fine* if it wasn't for you!" Eryn fumed. "She would be living the elven dream if she was not cursed with the kindest heart that God has ever seen. Is she dying because of you, witch? She saved your life, you said. *Is she dying because of you!?*"

"She did it for me, mom." Reya stepped between us. "I'm still in shock from it all, but Kieran got hurt trying to save me. And Mia. And a few others. And, mom, if it wasn't for Mia, Kieran would...she would...she'd be dead."

Shock struck Eryn's eyes. She glanced from me to Reya, searchin' for thah truth. "I need to know...exactly what happened." her eyes pleaded. "Will you tell me?"

"Of course." I guided her to a chaih.

Eryn sat down, still grippin' Reya's hand like a lifeline. She brushed teahs from her eyes and I fought down grief of my own.

"Thank you." she breathed.

I sat down an' sighed, tryin' to figuah out where to staht.

Please be okay, Kieran. Please.

Black Wolf – Aislyn

I stood outside the front door of my aunt's house. That's where this whole things started, with the Pack and the Gathering, and my own fears. I found it strange that I didn't feel them anymore. Yes, I had broken the tenets of the wolves' code, but I had been young, and murder breeds murder.

I jogged up the steps and knocked on the door. My aunt opened it, looking like she hadn't slept in days.

Has it only been days?

"I'm home." I said, locking my gaze with hers. I wouldn't be afraid of the wolves anymore.

"Aislyn!" she wrapped her arms around me.

I hugged her in return, grateful for someone who, at last, smelled of pack. She withdrew and scrutinized me, the stitches on my neck, the years inside my eyes.

"You smell of blood, magic, and death. Where have you been?"

I quirked my lips. "Heaven. Hell. All in between."

"Come inside." she bade me.

I stepped over the threshold and followed my aunt into the living room. Surprise thundered through me as the alpha turned and glared at me. My aunt bowed and bared her neck. I remained standing.

"What is the meaning of this?" he questioned.

I turned to my aunt. "Why is he here?" I ignored him.

"A missing wolf is something that warrants my attention." he answered before she could.

"Aislyn, show respect." my aunt hissed, and I could smell the fear on her.

I grew fed up with this culture, this life, this lie.

"I want lone wolf status." I said the words before I knew I wanted to say them.

"What!?" the question flew at me in unison.

Firm in my conviction, I spoke again. "I want lone wolf status."

"Aislyn, you are the weakest link in the pack." the alpha growled as he felt his authority challenged. "Do you really think you can best me in single combat?"

"I don't think I need to." I snapped, refusing to look away. I felt absolute peace.

"You know our laws, Aislyn. Do you think yourself above them?" the alpha snarled, baring his teeth as his eyes flashed amber.

"I know pack law." I replied. "And I know it is written in your hand. I serve no man, no wolf, and no curse. My God is above all of that."

The alpha, who had so long thought of the curse as his master, who worshipped his second form as holy, was stupefied. "Your god, puppy?"

"My God." I stood firm, smiling as I remembered Mia's less than witty repartee as the alpha got in my face, so close I could smell the raw meat on his breath. "Back the fuck off."

"You are banished from this house!" my aunt shrieked. "And from this family and..." she looked to the alpha for permission, something I would *never* do again.

"From this pack." he agreed. "A lone wolf is honorable. But you are banished, disgraced! Get out of here and know that you are the shame of your people!"

I turned on my heel and left the house, a lightness in my heart that had not been there since my childhood. I had no possessions, no money, and no home, but I had knowledge of the truth.

God is more forgiving of the past than men or angels. Forgiveness is love. Love is all that matters. Now to go and wait for the moon...and maybe meet a friend in the sunlight.

Coffee Shop Salvation – Judah

Eternity means nothing anymore. I look at the world through new lenses. Everything is washed in brighter light. I am in this light. For the first time in centuries, the sun kisses my skin.

I walked through the doors, hearing the bells jangle, inhaling the scent of coffee. Simple paradise. I smiled at the young girl behind the bar, ordered, and sat down at a table. Time ticked by and I cherished each moment.

Someone sat down before me and I turned my attention to them. Darrintek smiled and grasped at the air. A cup of coffee appeared in his hand.

"So I hear I will no longer be walking the ways of forever with you."

I smiled and felt it reach my eyes. "I am mortal again." I said. "Human. Do you know what that means?"

"It means you are free." he replied, gazing into the distance. "You belong to the mortal coil now. You are once more favored in the eyes of God."

I took a sip of my coffee and laughed when it burned my tongue. "I believe that it has been so long since either angels or demons saw the face of God that you have forgotten what it looks like."

"You were always so honest, Judah. Ever unafraid of blasphemy."

I shrugged and leaned back in my chair. "When blasphemy becomes truth, what then, Darrin? Do we deny it for the sake of old standards or embrace it for its truth?"

"Ever the philosopher." Darrin mused. "So tell me, what is the face of God?"

I thought of the elf bleeding on the floor, giving everything of herself for fragments of others. Blood had never before resembled redemption to me. Until now.

"The face of God is love. Nothing else, but nothing less."

Darrin glowered at me. "Angels and demons know nothing of love."

"I think you do." I countered. "And if not, you have an eternity to decipher its mysteries."

"Are you calling us fools?" he growled, anger striking his violet eyes.

"In a manner." I grinned. "But you cannot exact retribution from me, Darrin. I'm human once again."

The demon stood up. "Damn you, Judah."

"Someone tried that once before." I saluted him with my coffee cup. "As you can see, it did not work so well."

"Don't get cocky, Judah. Men are not yet free from the vagaries of Heaven. Not even men such as you."

I felt humbled. "You are right. I did not broker my salvation. But I do know what I have seen. It is a blasphemous truth. But it is true. Let it go, old friend."

"Old friend indeed." he nodded. "The four of you are enemies of heaven and hell."

"Of course. The doctors despise it when their lab rats escape. Farewell, Darrintek. I believe that now, at last, I have a life to lead."

"Live it well, Judah." he bade me.

I turned from him and left the coffee shop. A young woman with beautiful red hair and wolf's eyes caught my attention.

"I believe I will, Darrin." I smiled and ran to catch up with her.

I believe I will.

God in His Heaven – Kieran

The sound of my own heartbeat woke me. I slanted my eyes towards the noise and saw green light jumping on a monitor. There were tubes dangling above me and the back of my hand stung. Something hard and uncomfortable was forcing cold air up my nose and I tugged on it, disappointed to find my hands weak and uncoordinated.

"None of that, crazy elf." a familiar accent met my ears, and gentle, weary hands replaced the oxygen tube. "Ya still ain't breathin' like ya should."

"I hate hospitals." I croaked.

"Ya know, so do I." the mirth in her voice was forced. "Thah only reason I've been in one this fuckin' long is 'cause you wouldn't leave."

I gasp/laughed, feeling a deep pain behind the numb of medication. "Mia." I smiled.

"Welcome back to thah world." my witch traced my cheek with her fingertips. Her hands were warm.

"How long have I been away?" I asked.

She grinned. "Long enough to make me have several uncomftahble convahsations with ya mothah." her face fell. "I was fuckin' scared, Kieran."

"Why?" I wanted to take the sadness out of those mischievous blue eyes.

"They thought they got ya fixed thah first time." Mia brushed tears from her eyes. "Theah was a lotta fuckin' damage, Kieran. You were in surgery for seven hours…then they took ya to ICU. Four hours later…ya went intah cahdiac arrest. They…" she choked up, "they missed a little teah in ya artahry. You've been in a medically induced coma for a week."

"And you stayed?" I asked, hope filling my heart.

What was between us…it was so new, so different and so difficult to face. But she had remained beside me, caring for me, holding on to hope for me.

I saw the bandage wrapped around her hand and tears pricked my eyes.

"Yeah." her voice was low and rough, muted by emotion. "You're all I've got left in this world. My fam'ly won't have me an' no othah coven will adopt a blood witch. You're thah only hope I've got."

I reached out and she twined her fingers with my own. "I know the feeling." I pressed my free hand to my chest. "Here. I feel you here. You were my heartbeat, Mia...my lifeline. I love you."

"Really?" she smiled and wiped the tears from her cheeks. "'Cause ya ma tells me you were all set to marry some elven hotshot."

I sat up and gasped, feeling the pain that the meds held at bay roar at me with a ferocity unmatched. Mia caught me by the shoulders and eased me back against the pillows, making disapproving noises, though her eyes were filled with worry.

"F...fuck that." I breathed. "I didn't even know him. Besides...I love you. Elven tradition...can kiss my ass."

She reached up and tucked my hair behind my ears. "Don't evah freak me out like that again." she warned. "Thah war is ovah. Don't you go findin' anothah one to fight. 'Sides, something tells me we're gonna have enough of a battle tryin' to get ya mothah to accept this...whatevah it is."

I smiled, feeling a healing sleep beginning to tug at me. "I'm no warrior." I promised. "Not anymore. Do...do you know what happened to the others, Mia? Have you heard anything from them?"

"Nah. 'Xcept ya sistah, who is fine by the way. But we all went our sepahrate ways. Figuahed it was bettah like that. Ya nevah know if that Josephine bitch will keep her word."

"She will." I wondered if the pity I felt for her would ever leave. "She fell from heaven."

"What thah fuck?" the familiar question, and my quiet laughter. "Ya mean she's a demon now?"

"Yes. She gave up on love and heaven."

"Aftah all ya did for her? She gave up on love aftah seein' what you did? That's so fuckin' ridiculous."

"I know." I closed my eyes, tired. "But they have the luxury of time. We don't. In the end, I think we're all set to search for the same thing."

"Huh?"

"Fate Path." I licked my chapped lips. "It leads to love. That's all it's about. And my search is completed...not with war, or vengeance. But love."

Mia's hand stroked through my hair. "I think we're lucky. Do you?"

"Damn straight." I drifted further towards sleep.

"You tired, baby?" Mia asked, her rough accent etched with tenderness.

"Mm-hmm." I felt the medication begin pulling me away.

"G'night, Kieran." Mia whispered, and I felt the slightest brush of lips on my forehead. "I love you."

Here am I, on earth, I thought, bleary, *away from the machinations of those above and those below, set to live a mortal life. A life that will, against its design, end. But it will be a life lived in love. That's all that matters. Destiny is fulfilled.*

Here am I, on earth. God is in his Heaven.

It can stay that way.